THE LOST EDEN

STORM SONG

©Copyright 2020 Wicked Storm Publishing
This book is a work of fiction and is purely for entertainment. Any resemblance of names, places, or anything else is simply a coincidence.
All rights reserved.
Not for copy or resale

Chapter 1

Drowning. They say it's one of the most peaceful ways to die. It's said it's almost painless. You go quick, slip into eternal euphoria before you even realize what's happening.

Sitting at the bottom of the pool at Sister Mary's Reformatory for Water Mages for the hundredth time just seconds before my lungs cave in and inhale the sweet poison- I call bullshit.

My lungs burned like someone poured acid into them. My eyes ached and my throat was set ablaze. Even still, it was no comparison to the pain of the first time the nuns tossed me in with weights strapped to my legs. They were sure that I had the magic just like everyone else, I just needed to want it bad enough. Every day they threw me in, just to pull me out a few minutes later and use their magic to rip the water from my lungs. All to do it all again the next week.

To them it was better than the alternative, admitting that maybe I was just a magical dud, dropped on the doorstep of their all girls school. Not possessed, not cursed, just- me.

Every time I saw a body of water those feelings came back. It wasn't just the helplessness, it was the suffocation that crept into my lungs like a monster that I could never shake. It was the overwhelming feeling that I wasn't just inadequate, I was so unacceptable in a society where everyone could control one of the four elements that if I died in the process of them trying to activate my magic, it was an acceptable price to pay.

Now, staring into the sudsy dishwater, those feelings came rushing back.

"I hate water." I grumbled under my breath as I pulled out my hundredth coffee cup and shoved my cleaning brush inside of it.

"What was that Eden?" My manager Josh poked his head from around the corner with his signature passive aggressive smile plastered to his face.

Anxiety simmered inside my stomach. "Nothing. I'm almost done with the dishes."

"Great! I was just coming to tell you that we had a coffee emergency at table six, and we need you to bring the mop." He didn't even wait for a reply before he turned around and made his way back through the dark corridor and out into the main area of the coffee shop.

In hindsight, working at the mystical coffee shop that my best friend's rich parents had gifted her sounded a lot more fun than it was actually turning out to be.

I washed the last cup and set it up to dry before pulling the plug and watching the drain carry the muddy water out of sight. The swirl of the suds and the bubble of the drain made my skin crawl. I ripped my eyes from it and took a deep breath, drying my hands on my apron before grabbing the mop and slinking down the dark hallway.

I paused in the entryway that led to the cafe' from the kitchen and wiped a bead of sweat from my forehead. I leaned up against the wall and watched the baristas. I watched as they used their hands to bend and weave the water mixing it into coffee without laying a single finger on it. I watched one use his magic to pull a stream of iced latte out of the blender and it hovered in the air. A little girl watched in awe as he contorted it into the small shape of a horse, and made it gallop through the air before dropping into the coffee cup, squirting on some whipped cream, and throwing a lid on it. The girl squealed and clapped with glee and the mother slid a five dollar bill into the tip jar that sat perched on the counter.

I grabbed the mop and ripped my eyes from the counter, a twinge of jealousy coursing through my body.

I hated being a magical dud. I hated being the only one in the entire water caste, or any caste for that matter, that didn't have a single ability whatsoever.

Part of me truly felt like that was as far as my life would go, slopping a broom around in an old puddle of coffee.

I'd peaked. There wasn't much higher someone who was completely and utterly normal could go in a world filled with the extraordinary.

I twisted my mop in my mop bucket and tried not to think about it too much. I knew if I did it would just make me spiral into an existential crisis- again. And I was pretty sure my pillow was even sick of hearing me cry about the same things over and over again.

"Hey, Eden!" My eyes sprung up from the floor at the smooth, velvety sound of Trent Bishop's voice.

His baby blue eyes were locked directly on me. I tried my hardest not to swoon, but damn they were gorgeous.

I'd only been crushing on him since forever, and had yet to hear him actually say my name. To be honest I didn't even think he knew I existed, and my brain was prepared to enter full on panic mode.

Chill out, Eden. Just go see what he wants.

I talked myself out of a downward spiral. Even so, my legs refused to work, so I stood frozen, with my mouth hanging half open like an idiot.

"Uh, Eden?" Trent raised a brow.

"Yeah? Yeah. That's me, I'm Eden. Do you... Do you want me? I mean something! Not me, but something. What do you want?" I tripped over my words like a baby taking their first steps and died a little more inside with each one that left my lips.

Smooth. Real smooth.

Trent smiled, flashing the perfection that were his pearly white teeth, and his signature dimple caved in his left cheek.

Double swoon.

"Yeah, I've been meaning to ask you all day but I just didn't get a second to pull you aside." He rubbed at the back of his neck nervously.

This is it. The moment he finally professes his love for me. I quickly glanced down at the old food and coffee stains on my dingy apron. *Not the outfit I imagined I'd be wearing when Trent finally asked me out, but beggars can't be choosers.*

My stomach erupted with butterflies and I could feel my cheeks getting pinker by the second. I'd only been waiting for the moment for years, no biggie.

"You can ask me anything Trent." The words came out a little too eagerly than I'd meant for them to, but I couldn't shove them back into my mouth and try again so I just bit down on my lip and tried to let it go.

Trent leaned over the counter closer to me and I froze. He'd never been that close to me and all I could think about was how soft and pink his lips looked. How I wanted to run my fingertips across them while he swept me up in his arms and whisked me off to some back room without a care in the world.

How he would look with nothing but the scent of my body in him.

He leaned in as close as he could and whispered "The sink is backed up, and we need you to snake it." With a devilish smirk on his face.

Two of the other baristas burst out laughing from around the corner and my face went from pink to bright red.

"Oh my god, did you see her face?" Veronica, one of the classic mean blondes laughed. "She looked like she wet her panties the second you said her name."

Trent smiled. "As if I'd be interested in anyone but my spark." He pulled Veronica in and they commenced making out sloppily in the middle of the cafe'.

My heart sunk into the floor, but not before it shattered into a million pieces. I pulled my eyes from their atrocious display of public affection and they finally pulled their faces apart in time for Veronica to mouth *bye loser* before they clocked out and made their way out of the cafe.

I stood in front of the counter in awe, blinking the tears back in my eyes, but there wasn't much I could do for the golf ball sized lump that had grown in my throat.

"I'm sorry, are you in line to order?" A woman's voice came from behind me.

I spun around to see a cute looking couple waiting to order. The woman had her arm wrapped tenderly around the man's.

"Oh, no, sorry." I managed to get out before sliding out of the way.

I glanced around nervously as I made my way behind the counter and to the sink in the back, feeling like everyone's eyes were on me. Like everyone had witnessed my humiliation.

In times like these people normally would feel anger, or wrath, or the need for revenge.

But all I felt was sad. It was a horribly familiar feeling that seeped into the pit of my stomach where it usually called home.

I sulked to the sink and grudgingly pulled the long wire from the cabinet underneath it.

Behind me came the sound of laughter. I was so used to laughter being at my expense that I spun around out of pure instinct, the nervousness already rising inside me, but only found the woman from earlier gazing lovingly at the man.

There was a look of pure happiness in her eyes, one that his eyes lovingly reflected. They looked so happy, so carefree, so in love.

So why did that make me feel anxious?

"We just sparked right away. You know, it was meant to be." I heard her say over my shoulder.

I shoved the wire down into the drain with a little more disdain than I'd care to admit.

I'd spent my entire life dreaming of my spark. A spark was the magical equivalent of love at first sight, except it's powerfully fated magic tied your souls together. You only got one, and once you got it, it was impossible to ignore.

My spark was all I had left to look forward to in life.

I didn't have family, I didn't have tons of money or a fancy job. I didn't even have a lick of magic. My spark was the only prospective thing in my life that I hadn't screwed up. And I was waiting for it on pins and needles since the moment I knew what it was.

They said it felt like a tingle in your eyes, or a vibrating in your chest. Either way, when you sparked with someone you knew. There was no mistaking it.

I shook the wire around in the drain until the sink full of dirty water started to drain.

Thank god.

I looked at my watch, it was five thirty, thirty minutes late to clock out again. And I knew Josh hated approving overtime. I did get a little leeway because I was roommates with the owner, but still.

"I'm heading out." I yelled to Josh over the clank of coffee cups. I hung up my apron and slid my timecard through the slot.

I knew that I wasn't completely finished with the absurd amount of work he'd piled on me for the day, and that I'd never hear the end of it in the morning but I silently prayed he'd give me a break because it would be my birthday.

But probably not.

I slid on my jacket and pulled my winter hat over my ears before pushing through the front door. I clutched the thick novel I was reading closely to my body, it was a limited edition and I was damned if I was going to let anything damage it. We were in late spring, but a cold front still lingered, sweeping through the city every now and then.

I shoved my hands in my pockets and made my way down the sidewalk, silently grateful that the house Jade and I stayed in was only a few blocks away. For the most part I kept my eyes down, focusing only on putting one foot in front of the other, but I especially honed in on the ground when someone walked by. Eye contact made my skin crawl, especially out in the wild. I could barely stomach it in the shop.

I turned a corner and some kids playing in the water across the street caught my eye. They had to be about five years old playing with a water hose. I shivered at the thought of the cold water they played in. I didn't know how they could do it, but they did.

I watched as one of the kids held their hands in front of it and was able to bend the stream ever so slightly.

I sighed and moved on.

Everyone in the water caste could manipulate the element on some level. Whether it was being able to lift a drop of water all the way up to being able to lift entire boats out to the ocean and everything in between.

Everyone but me.

It made me feel so far beyond lonely.

Centuries ago the elemental mages appeared out of society, at first little by little. No one knew why, but over the course of a year everyone in the world had been *gifted* an ability to manipulate an element. Water, fire, air, and earth.

As you can imagine, the tensions grew between the different types of mages. Fights broke out between water and fire mages who were neighbors.

Earth and Air mages grew to hate one another. As with anything that makes people different it caused a rift in society as people grew ever loyal to their own type of elemental magic. Thus, the caste system was born. The country was divided into four kingdoms, one for each element, and mages were relocated according to which type of magic coursed through their veins. It helped cut down the tensions, but only made the loyalty and nationalism towards castes even greater.

But among all that, I didn't know where I fit. I didn't belong anywhere, and it felt like nobody wanted me.

No one but Jade.

"Hey girl, how was work?" Jade's blonde head poked out of the kitchen as I slid through the front door of our house.

"It was okay." I lied, sliding my jacket from my shoulders and hanging my hat in its place.

Jade was perfect. She was rich, popular, and had a handsome fiancé who she sparked with when they were thirteen. I loved her, and she loved me, but she didn't understand my struggles. Not a single bit.

I took in a deep breath and the smell of warm lasagna filled my nostrils, dulling the sadness I felt inside.

"You got here just in time for the first bite." She smiled.

I smiled too.

We ate dinner while she told me about the amazing date Charles had planned for her, and I watched the excitement in her eyes with only a twinge of guilt, and a whole lot of sadness.

"What's wrong?" Jade stopped mid-sentence.

"Nothing, I'm just having a crappy day." I said with tears in my eyes.

Jade smiled. "It's a good thing I have everything set up for our girl's night then, huh?"

She led me into the small living room. Flashing lights were strung on the ceiling, an assortment of snacks were laid out on the coffee table, and my favorite movie was set to play on the TV.

"This is literally the best." I smiled.

It's too bad that I didn't know that was literally the best my life would be for a long time.

Chapter 2

I stepped out on the small front porch in the wee hours of the morning. The rain poured down around me and the memories started to creep back in.

Why the heck do you have to say yes to everyone Eden? I grumbled.

The brisk morning air stung my face and a deep breath shared the pain with my lungs. A small puff of smoke rose from my mouth and dissolved into the air.

This is what I get for agreeing to open the brew today. A shiver ran down my spine at the cold.

Jade had asked me the night before if I'd take her shift opening the coffee shop, right before she left to spend the night with Charles. The last thing I wanted to do was drag myself out of the comfort of my warm bed at the crack of dawn and freeze on the mile walk to the shop, but there I was.

Jade was the only person in the world that I really cared about- the only friend I'd ever known. Rain or shine, I'd be there for her. She took pity on me all those years ago when I was just the lonely orphan charity case that our elite academy adopted, and we'd been friends ever since.

I forced my eyes away from the downpour and fumbled with my keys before they slipped from my hands and spiraled to the ground. I let out a tired sigh and bent down to snatch them.

Nearby a twig snapped loudly over the rush of the rain, leaving a jolt of hairs raised on the back of my neck. My eyes immediately darted to the tall bushes outside the house. They were as tall as a large person and call me crazy but it was secretly a fear of mine that one day someone would take advantage of the shelter that they provided as a hiding place.

I jumped up with the keys clutched tightly in my hand.

"Jade? Is that you?" I tried my best not to let my words come out laced with fear.

Silence.

I let out a chuckle and brushed it off as a byproduct of the nightmares that I'd been having for the past week. The same nightmares I had every week leading up to my birthday for as long as I could remember. I should have been used to it, but every year they felt more intense. They were so vivid and real that sometimes I woke up screaming drenched in sweat. They were the kind that scared you not because of the monsters that were chasing you, but because the monster that they made you feel like.

Every year it was the same, first came the dream of the family trapped in a house that I set on fire myself. Then came the dream where I drove a car into a bridge with an innocent person in the back seat, forced to watch her drown. After that was the earthquake dream, where the entire city was swallowed by a crater in the ground and I watched it crushed by a rock slide. Then to top off came the tornado dream where I watched everything I love ripped from the earth and carried far away by the vicious winds.

They always came a week before my birthday like clockwork.

They lined up one by one leading to my big day, when I was finally blessed not to have a single dream, good or bad, for another year until the cycle decided to begin again.

My cellphone vibrated inside my pocket with a text from that read

Just want to make sure you're awake and didn't forget that you volunteered to open the brew for me today. Love you. xoxo

I let out a snort at the fact that her idea of volunteering involved immense peer pressure and guilt tripping. But she was one of those people that you couldn't help but love no matter how blunt they were. Secretly I'd always admired it about her. She told people like it was, and if she didn't want to do something she'd let you know it.

More importantly she wouldn't have agreed to open up the brew if she didn't feel like it, so I was especially envious of her truth telling abilities at that moment.

I slid the phone back into my pocket and started to run through the list of steps to open the brew. By the time I made my way down the walkway and onto the sidewalk the noise in the bushes was the furthest thing from my mind.

As I walked I watched the rising sun blanket everything in the dim morning light. The apartment windows glistened in its rays, and even the dewdrops on the grass sparkled. That was the only thing that made getting up early to be Jade's errand girl worth it. I loved the stillness and the serenity that being the only person awake gave me. I didn't have to hide, I didn't have to pretend, I could just be part of nature. Birds chirped and flew over my head as they began to wake too.

I smiled up at them, admiring their freedom to roam wherever they wanted. There were so many times that I wished I could just fly away and disappear to a far off land. One where I'd have a purpose in life besides trying to hide the fact that I didn't have one.

Behind me there was the sudden crash of a trash can hitting the pavement that made me jolt back to reality.

I stopped in my tracks in the middle of the sidewalk and looked around anxiously. Slowly the feeling of being watched washed over me in waves, getting more and more intense with every second that passed. I scanned the road behind me. A trash can lay on its side. I didn't know if my eyes were playing tricks on me, but for a second

I swore that it was smoldering like it held something hot inside. The heat lines rose up from it, skewing my vision of everything behind it.

I took a step closer, overcome by the sudden urge to get answers but something fell from the sky and landed in front of me with a thud. I looked down to see a bird, burnt to a crisp. It's charred body nearly reduced to ash by the impact.

I immediately felt sick to my stomach at the smell of its burning flesh. I spun around and ran, it was all I could think to do in the moment. My brain barely had time to process what was happening. My heart thudded in my chest so loudly that it drowned out my thoughts and replaced them with pure adrenaline. I swore I heard footsteps behind me closing in, but I refused to look back. I ran through the empty streets, praying that I'd meet someone on the sidewalk and they would tell me that I was crazy, and probably needed sleep. I wouldn't even have cared if they would have called the police on me and I had to spend a night in jail for disturbing the peace. All I wanted to know was that I was safe.

My fingers fumbled in my pocket until I got a grasp on my phone. I tried to hold it steady enough to unlock and typed Jade's number by heart.

Behind me I heard another trash can meet an untimely death.

So I didn't imagine it.

The phone line continued to ring and I took a sharp left into the back alley behind the town's supermarket. Once I made it all the way to the other side of the street I took a sharp right and dipped into the shadows of the movie theater alley. A pain stabbed into my side with every sharp gasp I took for air.

That's it. I'm finally going to work out. Cross my heart and hope to-

There was a low snarl next to the building that cut off my train of thought. It didn't sound like an animal, and it definitely didn't sound human. I clamped my hand tightly over my mouth and took shallow breaths. At that point my heart was racing so fast that if I didn't know better I would have thought it wasn't beating at all. Footsteps slowly thundered their way in my direction. Whatever it was, it knew I was close and I had a feeling that it wasn't going to stop until it got what it wanted.

Me.

But why? There was absolutely nothing under the sun that made me special.

It inched closer and closer, closing in the little space between us. Every hair on my body stood on end. I shut my eyes as tight as I could and a single tear ran down my cheek. My breathing was staggered and low, but I didn't know how much longer I could take before my lungs betrayed me and filled themselves.

Just as whatever beast it was got to the corner of the alleyway there was a loud noise that crashed around the corner. Without a second of hesitation I heard it retreat back up the sidewalk and disappear.

I unclamped my mouth and took in gulps of air.

What the hell was that thing?

I had no idea what was going on. There was part of me that was convinced I was actually still sleeping and my subconscious just decided to add another nightmare to the birthday line up.

Despite almost dying I couldn't shake the feeling of familiarity. I didn't know why, and I didn't know how, but some part of my brain was comfortable with the chaos.

All I knew was that I needed to get out of the open and somewhere safe where I could get my head straight.

I scurried out of the alley and quickly made my way toward the Mystic brew. I let out a sigh of relief when it's neon pink sign came into view. Whatever beast it was, was gone but the overwhelming feeling that I wasn't alone stuck to me like glue. I felt eyes on me, an invisible force calculating every move. To me that was almost worse.

I quickly rummaged in my pocket and pulled out the old set of skeleton keys that belonged to the building and flipped to the bright yellow one that unlocked the front door. My fingers trembled. I tried to calm them but no matter how hard I tried I couldn't. The feeling that something else was coming overwhelmed every sense I had. Something I couldn't control. The trash can, the bird, none of it made any sense. Even Jade not answering her phone when she had just sent me a text was weird. Everything about it was off, and if it was any indicator about how my twentieth year of life was going to go I was ready to crawl under my bedsheets and sleep until twenty one came.

I finally managed to slip the key into the lock and a wave of relief came over me. I quickly pulled the door open and scurried inside locking it behind me. I peered through the blinds that covered the vintage glass door and eyed everything outside suspiciously, which wasn't anything at all.

Maybe it really is all in my head. My heart began to slow. *Maybe it's getting bad again.*

I flinched at the thought of the repeated psychotic episodes I went through when I was twelve- imagining things that weren't there, mumbling nonsensical things, the paranoia that someone out there was out to get me. It had taken years and years of therapy and magical drugs to get me to the place I was at. My sanity was something I'd worked hard for and I wasn't about to let anything else catch me by surprise.

I flipped the light switch on and the boom of a confetti cannon exploded in my face. I screamed at the top of my lungs as my coworkers jumped out from behind the counter and yelled "Surprise!"

I froze with a look of horror stuck on my face as they charged toward me with party hats and balloons.

"What are you guys doing here?" I asked through the gritted teeth behind my smile.

Josh put a party hat on top of my head, like he hadn't just cussed me out the day before over spilled coffee on the cafe floor. He held his usual stiff smile strongly.

"What do you mean what are we doing here? Jade set this all up. Did you think that she'd really forget your birthday?."

My ears perked up. If Jade was there that meant one last thing I needed to kill myself with anxiety over. She was safe.

And maybe she could help me figure out what the hell was going on.

"She was going to meet us here though. Looks like she's running later than you for once." Josh added.

Crap.

Chapter 3

C ome on, pick up. Pick up.

The phone rang a few times before going to Jade's voicemail.

"Hey it's me again. I just wanted to say thanks for the surprise, I think, but answer your phone. I'm worried. Things are-" I paused, wondering if it was even worth mentioning. What's a small psychotic break after all? "Just call me back, please. We're about to open."

I hung up the phone and took a sharp inhale. In times like that my anxiety threatened to take the reins, and I'd had enough mental breakdowns for one day. I got up from the small toilet in the employee bathroom and stood in front of the dirty mirror.

I ran my fingers through my long brown waves and fixed the nametag on my hot pink work apron. My eyes locked onto my reflection.

"Why can't you ever get your shit together." I scowled.

There was a knock at the door.

"Just a minute!" I scrambled to turn on the faucet, and hoped that whoever it was didn't hear me talking to myself like a loon.

The water spurted out of the faucet fast and hard. I reached underneath the spout to wash my hands and the water bent in an odd way, avoiding my hands completely like a magnet avoiding another.

What the heck is going on today?

I pulled my hands from the sink and tried again. This time instead of bending around my hands the force completely defied gravity and pushed the water up the opposite direction and forced the stream directly into my face.

I let out a scream at the blast of hot water in my eyes.

"What the hell!" I screamed out, no longer able to hold in my frustration.

The knock came from the door again.

"Just a minute! I'm in here!" I yelled angrily, but immediately regretted it.

I grabbed a handful of paper towels and opened the door to apologize for being rude. A stunned customer stood in front of me.

He was taller than me, but I guessed that he was around the same age. His hair was a deep shade of red, and he had a maroon colored scar that ran diagonally through his left eye. It was the kind of thing that you noticed right away, hard to forget, but strangely it didn't take away from his charm. He was attractive, and that was the sort of thing that made me even more nervous about the situation.

"Are you okay?" He asked. His voice was smooth and devoid of emotion. If anything he just sounded bored.

"Yeah I just, uh, was on the phone." I could feel my cheeks burning red.

His green eyes stared into mine and he clenched his sharp jaw tightly before nodding.

I stood in the doorway still mesmerized. There was something about him that was- different. Something I couldn't quite put my finger on. It wasn't just how gorgeous he was, either. Something lingered beneath the surface of my mind, begging to be remembered.

"Are you done with the bathroom?" He raised a brow at me frozen in my place. "That guy told me to use this one because the other one was broken."

"Yeah Yeah Yeah. Right." I made a fool of myself.

He took a step forward and so did I. Instead of turning to the side to let him pass I crashed right into him like a fool. The second our bodies touched it was like my head screamed. A sharp pain seared into it, like a poker fresh from the flames. I doubled over and grabbed my head. I saw fire, everywhere. It spread as far as the eye could see. It climbed up the walls, and ate away at the ceilings.

"Hey are you okay?" His voice pulled me back to reality.

The fire and the pain were gone. All that was left in their place was him, standing in the doorway with an uneasy look on his face.

"I'm fine." I mumbled in a blaze as I scrambled to my feet by myself.

He shrugged his shoulders and closed the bathroom door. My head throbbed and every sound made me feel like my vision was going to blur. It didn't hurt, but something inside of it just didn't feel right.

"There she is! The birthday girl has returned!" Josh threw his hands in the air. "Just in time. Go take your place behind the counter, a line's already started to form outside."

"Behind the counter?" I asked in confusion, ready to throw on my kitchen apron and disappear into the back room where they usually kept me.

"Yes. Jade's orders, today you get to be a barista."

I would have been slightly elated, but the way Josh ate the words as they came out of his mouth killed it all for me. He didn't want me behind the counter, and I doubted that any of the other baristas did either.

But once again Jade used her powers of rich persuasion to get what she wanted, and this time it benefitted me.

I forced a smile and made my way behind the counter, awkwardly waiting for direction. All the others stared on, and I caught a glimpse of Trent whispering something to Veronica. She busted out laughing before she made eye contact with me and whispered something back to him.

My stomach sank.

As if a psychotic break wasn't enough, I had to be ridiculed too.

I tried to push everything out of my mind.

Josh unlocked the door and a wave of customers made their way inside. The Mystic Brew wasn't just popular in our town, it was one of the most well known magical coffee shop franchises throughout the entire water caste. People gravitated to it for it's hot pink decor and killer magical branding, but also because of the show that the baristas put on.

I stood waiting for direction when Josh finally pulled me to the blender and handed me an ice scoop.

That was my birthday gift. I got to scoop ice, then blend it.

Fun.

One of the baristas handed me a coffee that needed blending and as I started pouring it my phone started to buzz in my pocket.

Crap crap crap.

I tried to pour it as quickly as I could but by the time the cup was empty the buzzing had stopped.

Might as well just finish the order now. I groaned and blended it.

"Here you go." I said with a smile as I handed it back to the barista who would get all the credit, and as a result, all of the tip.

I turned my back for a second and slipped my phone out of my pocket. It was Jade.

"Phone away Eden." Josh scolded.

"Yeah I'm sorry." I apologized. "It won't happen again."

My cheeks tingled. I didn't like being reprimanded at work. It made my stomach hurt just thinking that someone thought I wasn't doing a good enough job. It seemed small and meaningless, but it was the way my anxiety functioned. So I promised myself that I wouldn't pull it out again until all the customers were out, per Josh's policy.

I plastered my signature smile back on my face and did my job. Coffee, ice, blend. Coffee, ice, blend.

I'd blended so much that my hands shook from all the vibrations. The line was so long that it took 15 minutes to clear it. Most of the customers took their coffee to go, but we still had one or two stragglers who regularly decided to sit down to read or work on their laptops.

"Can I check my phone now Josh?" I asked as politely as I could. "Jade called and I wanted to see if she left a message or not."

"Why didn't you say so? She was supposed to be here before opening to work a barista shift, now we're one short. Ask her if I need to call in a replacement."

I nodded and moved to the small hallway off to the side that led to the employee bathroom and break room. My phone screen lit up and showed two missed calls from Jade and a voicemail.

Oh thank god. I breathed a sigh of relief. *Hopefully she'll tell me where the heck she is.*

I brought the phone to my ear but all I heard was heavy breathing and a lot of rustling around, like she was running. It went on for a few seconds before she ever said a word.

"Eden, I need you to pick up your damn phone right now. " She said between large gasps for air. "Something's wrong. Everything is all fucked up." I could tell she'd been crying by the way her voice shook. "I think someone's after me but I don't -" Her words were cut off by her blood curdling scream. It was so loud it made my eardrum pulsate and I had to pull the phone from my ear.

My stomach dropped into my shoes and my heart started to race in my chest.

I hit the call back button and it went straight to voicemail.

Crap.

Redial- voicemail.

Double crap.

I didn't know what to do besides call her fiance Charles, which went straight to voicemail too.

Jade's parents were away on vacation somewhere in the mountains with no cell service, and I knew from experience that the authorities wouldn't take it seriously until she'd been missing for a few days. I'd watched enough cop shows to know that.

I walked back to the counter in a daze.

The baristas chatted and laughed with one another as they practiced their water magic. It was too much for me, every noise overstimulated me and pushed me an inch closer to the edge.

I needed someplace quiet where I could sort out my thoughts and figure out what to do next. What the hell was going on this birthday? Was the universe finally trying to catch up on all the bad karma that I'd only narrowly escaped growing up?

Way to throw it all on at once, universe.

The bell that chimed when the front door was opened went off and a group of customers walked in, a family with a bunch of kids.

I knew from years of experience that when kids got involved, orders got complicated.

Ice, no ice. Blended a little, blended a lot. Were we sure we extracted every trace of caffeine and sugar from their child's completely caffeinated and sugar laced drink? I took one look at the mother and knew that it was going to be too much for me to even overhear. I couldn't take it, not in the state that I was in.

"I need to use the bathroom." I whispered to Josh. "Do you know if that guy is still in there?"

"What guy?" Josh looked at me out of the side of his eye.

"The customer that you told to use the employee bathroom because the customer one was broken. Tall, dark, big red mark streaked across his face. Ring a bell? He'd be a hard one to miss."

Josh shook his head. "I definitely didn't see anyone like that. You were here when we opened the doors. You saw all the customers that came in just when I did."

Oh no. The psychotic breaks must be worse than I thought.

I felt my face turn white. "Yeah, right. I just need a little break." I didn't even wait for his permission before I turned around and made my way down the hall.

My head was spinning. Was I really slipping that bad? I'd only stopped taking the medicine that my therapist had given me for a week, but she was very adamant that these things could happen if I missed even one day. She said I had issues that only medication could solve, and that's why the social workers had me on them from a really young age and made me take them like clockwork.

Lesson learned. I was never going to skip another dose again.

The second I stepped foot in the hall I smelled it, a whiff of smoke. It hit my nostrils just as I pressed my hand up against the smooth wood door. I recoiled at the heat that came from it, clutching my aching hand close to my chest.

"Fire!" I yelled.

Everyone turned to look at me like I was insane. They barely had time to process.

"There's a fire!" I yelled, more angrily this time.

The woman at the counter grabbed one of her kids and just as she was about to bolt in the opposite direction there was a deafening boom.

Everything went black.

Chapter 4

My ears rang and my head throbbed. I winced at the sharp pain in my back where I'd landed.

I tried to catch the breath that had been knocked out of me but my lungs erupted in a fit of coughing at all the smoke I'd inhaled. I forced my eyes open and sat up.

"Holy crap." My mouth hung open.

I was completely surrounded by smoldering debris. Where the Mystic brew once stood now lay a pile of ash.

"Josh?" I got to my feet and waived a cloud of smoke away from my face.

There was nothing left. No bodies, no tables, not even the walls withstood the blast.

So how the hell did I?

My heart wrenched at the thought of the woman and her kids who last stood in front of the counter, and every barista that was there that day. Tears streamed down my cheeks leaving lines in my soot smeared face.

Then my mind turned to the stranger with the mark on his face. Had he shared the same demise?

Was he even ever there?

My mind was reeling with more questions than I had time to search for answers for. Suddenly I remembered the phone in my pocket and hoped that whatever saved me from being burned to a crisp saved it too.

"Oh thank god!" I pulled it from my pocket and kissed the screen. It lit up and showed another voicemail from Jade.

I breathed a sigh of relief because it meant that at least she wasn't dead. My hands shook as I brought the phone up to my ear. I couldn't tell if my ears were still recovering from the blast or she was just whispering but I was able to make out most of what she'd said.

"Eden, I need you to listen to me. You need to run. I hope you're not at the brew right now, just run. He's almost here, I can't run anymore. But you can. Don't trust anyone, I love you. Goodbye."

The voicemail looped from the beginning again.

What the hell is going on?

I rushed to dial for the police.

"Hello, I need help. There's been a fire, and there are a lot of people dead." My words slowly morphed into sobs. "And my friend Jade is missing. I think she might be dead too." I choked on the words as they came out.

By then a small crowd had started to form. Everyone's eyes were wide, and they were on me.

Some men ran up and siphoned some of the dew from the grass and water from a broken pipeline and used their magic to guide it to hot spots and put out the spreading fire.

I let my arm drop to my side, and my phone tumble from it into the smoldering ash before the officer on the line could even get a word in. I stared off into the distance. I didn't know what to do or who to turn to. How would I even explain something like this to the cops?

They would take one look at my mental history and label me an arsonist, then I'd never be able to help Jade. I felt myself slowly retreat back into myself like I did every other time life was too much for me to bear on my shoulders. I was disconnecting from the world- checking out from my emotions, and I knew once I did that I wouldn't be any help to Jade either.

It was a lose lose situation all around for the both of us.

A stranger charged toward me. His hair was a pale shade of aqua and he wore it so short that a lock of it nearly stuck straight up. His eyes were almost as blue as his hair. They were the first thing that stood out to me from inside the hood of his black hoodie. "Thank fuck you're okay. The Temple of Eden would have had my ass if you were killed on my watch."

His voice snapped me back to reality.

"The what?" I took a step back to put some distance between him and I trying to process what the hell that even meant.

At that point the crowd had grown but all of their attention was on the fires that were growing out of control and spreading to other buildings. No matter how much water they used nothing could quench the thirst of the flames as they ravaged through the old foundations.

"That doesn't matter right now. What matters is that you're coming with me right now."

Don't trust anyone. Jade's words rang in my mind, bouncing around aimlessly.

I assumed that also included handsome strangers.

"No I'm not." It was a simple, small act of defiance but it took all of my courage to muster. I wasn't the type of person that said no, ever, especially to strangers.

"I'm sorry, it's my fault for making it sound like you had a choice." His tone shifted immediately and he stood up straight.

I didn't know why but my first instinct was to run. Just as the cop cars made their way up the street I bolted in the opposite direction.

Behind me I heard the guy groan. I didn't know where I was going, or if anywhere was even safe for me anymore, but all I knew was the situation was impossible. I needed some control otherwise my anxiety would eat me alive.

What could I control in this situation?

Running.

I ran as fast and as hard as I could, praying that no one noticed me fleeing the scene. The flames were so uncontrollable they'd be occupied with them for a while before they calmed themselves and had time to think about survivors.

I ran faster and further than my lungs cared to let me before I collapsed in an exhausted heap on the sidewalk far from the brew. The pavement stung my palms as they scraped against it. I heaved and my lungs screamed at me but I felt a sense of satisfaction that I'd lost the mysterious stranger. I tried to focus on the sting in my lungs, or the hurt in my hands. Anything that could distract me from what was happening. I was on the verge of spiraling and I knew it better than I cared to admit.

I had no idea what to do next, or where to go but I knew one thing- I had to find Jade. She was the only friend I had in the world, the closest thing that I had to a family member. I wasn't going to abandon her, no matter how scared or overwhelmed the craziness made me feel.

Beside me there was a bubbling sound that gurgled in the storm drain embedded into the cement of the sidewalk.

"Oh what now?" I groaned.

Suddenly a burst of water rushed up from the drain and contorted into an odd shape. Before I knew it, it had morphed and taken the shape of the stranger I'd been running from.

"Really? Is that cheating?" I said between heaves. "Because I think that's cheating."

He couldn't help but smirk as he towered above me revealing

deep dimples in each cheek. His blue hair nearly glistened in the early morning light.

"I say if you got it, use it."

I pulled myself from the ground and hobbled away in the opposite direction.

A loud splash came from behind me as the water hit the sidewalk and another human shaped blob surfaced from a drain in front of me.

"Wow, you really are a stubborn one, aren't you?" He crossed his arms disapprovingly. Even though the fabric of his sweatshirt wasn't thin, I could tell his arms were thick and muscular.

I had a strong suspicion that he wasn't used to people telling him no. I wasn't used to saying it either, but right then nothing mattered to me except making sure Jade was safe.

"Look, I'm really sorry. I just need to go. I don't know what's going on or who you are but I need to find my friend." I took a step forward but he blocked my path. "I get it. You're some all powerful mage. You know a lot of fancy tricks, but none of that can help me. So please, if you don't mind could you stalk someone else?"

"You're not listening! I can help you find Jade." He huffed, annoyed that the situation was growing out of his control.

My feet planted into the sidewalk and I froze in place.

"How do you know her name?" I didn't bother turning around. I was ready to run the second his answer didn't sit right with me.

Another perk of having such horrible anxiety, you learned how to read people. Every subtlety about them was studied. I trusted my gut, if it said I had to run I'd run so far and so fast he'd have to track me down and drag my exhausted body through the city.

"Because at first I thought that she was the one I was here for." He groaned, almost embarrassed at the statement.

"What the hell do you mean?" I spun around. "What are you some super stalker?"

"No, just a guy who spent the last five years trying to track you down on behalf of your mother." His words sat heavy in my chest.

"I don't have a mother. You have the wrong girl." With that I turned and made my way down the sidewalk.

The mere mention of my biological parents made my skin crawl. They'd left me on the steps of an orphanage at the age of three with nothing but the clothes on my back and a baby blanket that had my name embroidered into it. I'd spent the rest of my childhood missing them as the memories of them faded, and the rest of my teenage years hating them for abandoning me. Only time could tell how I would spend my adult years, it was still up in the air. Some days it still stung just thinking of them. Other days I felt fine.

Healing from trauma was weird like that.

"You did, once. And she told me that when I found you I needed to mention the dreams."

I nearly tripped over my own feet when the words found their way out of his mouth.

"The what?" I turned back to him, and tried to act unbothered.

"The dreams. She said if you didn't believe me, that would do it. The elemental dreams. Fire, water, earth, and air." His eyes shifted around but it wasn't out of nerves, it was out of anger. Like my questions were an inconvenience to him. It wasn't safe to talk about out in the open like we were.

"What do you know about them?" I asked quickly. This time I was the one closing in on him. I didn't mean to come off as desperate for answers as I had, but just the thought of getting them about the mystery was enough to give me a sliver of hope, and hope was a dangerous thing for me to have. I knew from experience the damage to the heart that could come from that single sliver. Even still I was hungry for the truth, something that I had always felt was just out of my grasp. Taunting me.

"Oh now you believe me." He huffed. "We can't talk here. It's not safe. You're coming with me and I can explain on the way."

He turned and started back up the sidewalk, expecting me to follow him. I almost did, too, so used to going where people told me.

"No. Come back to my apartment with me." My face grew red at my own boldness.. "I have to see if Jade's there."

He spun around and raised a brow at me. The look on his face screamed that it was an idiotic idea. I could tell that he was there for me, and me only. Nothing else mattered to him.

But Jade mattered to me. I needed to find her. So I used myself as leverage for his help.

"Then you'll willingly come with me?" He raised a brow.

I made an X over my heart with my fingertip.

"Fine."

Chapter 5

He followed me through the streets, sure not to let me out of his sight. He even kept up as I bobbed and weaved my way through the alleys and took shortcuts to make it to the building in time.

"My name's Apollo, by the way." He groaned as we made it to the front porch. "Apollo Reef. Not that you care."

I shushed him and my eyes fixated on the front door, that hinged open just a crack. It was such a minuscule amount that no one else would have noticed, maybe I wouldn't have either if I hadn't dropped my keys that morning, cementing the fact that I locked the door completely in my mind.

"Something's not right."

"Yeah I'll tell you what it is, you're too stubborn to know when someone is trying to help you." He groaned.

I tried to shake off his words. Now wasn't the time to fall into one of my soul searching *maybe everyone's right about me* episodes.

I slowly nudged the door open with my foot and a squeaking noise pierced the silent air. I groaned at the fact that Jade still hadn't oiled the hinge despite the fact that I'd been telling her to for weeks. And look what happened, if there was a killer inside they definitely knew without a shadow of doubt that we were coming.

I added that to the list of gripes in my mind that I swore I'd hash out with her, but secretly knew I never would.

There was a bubbling noise behind me, and I turned to see Apollo had summoned some water from a pouch on his side and morphed it into the shape of a sword. He followed me closely ready to pounce at any moment. I could tell from the glint in his aqua eyes and the somber look on his face that this wasn't his first time charging into an unknown battle.

Who the hell are you? I caught myself wondering as I slowly tiptoed inside the quiet entryway.

The thick layer of silence that hung over the house was so eerie that it was almost hair raising. It didn't sit right with me, unsettled me deep inside. I knew something was wrong, I just didn't want to admit it to myself. Because if I did that meant that someone would have to fix it, and I was afraid that someone would end up being me.

I felt helpless through it all. I couldn't silence the nagging thought in the back of my mind that if I had water magic like everyone else maybe I would have been able to stop the explosion from ever happening. Or at least prevented some of the people from dying. I felt sick to my stomach every time I thought about the innocent customers who would never be going home to their families.

Even as I inched my way inside I felt useless. Apollo had his sword and his abilities, I had no idea what I expected to do if someone was actually inside.

Anxiety them to death? Because so far that seemed to be the only ability I had.

Focus Eden, Jade needs you. I nagged myself.

My heart raced faster as the door fully opened and my jaw dropped. The entire house was trashed from floor to ceiling.

Shattered pieces of glass lay scattered across the wooden floor from the picture frames that had been ripped from the walls. The closet beside the front door had been completely emptied and its contents were ripped to shreds. I slowly picked up a baseball bat from the rubble and held it out shakily.

"Yeah because that's definitely going to keep you safe." Apollo mumbled.

I wanted to tell him where he could shove all of his opinions, but just like every other time I wanted desperately to tell people to fuck off, I couldn't bring myself to do it.

I slowly stepped over the mess, sure to avoid the jagged shards of glass, and inched my way towards the living room. The couch was completely overturned, the TV was shattered, and all of the potted plants that Jade insisted on putting on the fireplace mantle were completely destroyed.

Whoever was here was clearly looking for something, but what? What could we possibly have had that was of any value to anyone?

Sure Jade had some pretty over the top things, but that just came with the territory of being a spoiled rich kid. But why would they be looking for them in the potted plants and inside the cushions of the couch?

I crept baseball bat first into the kitchen, hoping that Apollo wouldn't notice how much it was trembling. The truth was that I wouldn't even know how to use it as a weapon if my life depended on it. I was really just hoping that they'd see it, think that I meant business, and move along to a different house to loot.

It made enough sense in my mind to keep me putting one foot in front of the other.

My heart thudded inside my chest as I fumbled around in the dark for the light switch. It slowly sputtered on and my eyes adjusted. The fridge hung open and there was food strung across the room.

"What the hell were they looking for?" I finally said out loud.

At the sound of my voice there was a thud upstairs. It sounded like it was coming from Jade's bedroom.

"Jade?" I yelled out. "Jade is that you?" I bolted toward the staircase.

"Oh come on, you can't be that stupid can you?" Apollo shouted from across the house as he dashed to keep up with me. I was already halfway up the stairs by the time he assumed his place behind me muttering "I stand corrected. You can, and are."

"Next time tell me what the hell you're doing so I can tell you it's a stupid idea." He huffed.

He's really freaking bossy for someone who just met me. I groaned.

If Jade was there she would have put him in his place. She would have told him to fuck off and buy another box of hair dye for his gorgeous blue locks. If she was feeling particularly feisty she might have even told him that he could take that shiny magical sword and shove it up his ass.

But she wasn't there.

I sunk my teeth into my bottom lip, a tick I had whenever I was nervous, and slowly made my way up the stairs. The light bulb that normally lit the hallway was smashed to pieces, resulting in a lot of dark shadows that stretched along the hallway.

A dim flickering light shone from underneath Jade's doorway.

You have to go in there. I tried to force myself, despite the crippling sense of fear that coursed through my veins as thick as the blood that did too. *Jade needs you.*

"I'll check the other rooms first, just to make sure no one's hiding in them." I whispered to Apollo before I realized that I was doing exactly what he wanted me to do by giving him a play by play. "Not like it's any of your business." My warm cheeks tingled at the statement.

I turned away from him quickly. I refused to let him see how hard it was for me to even stand up to him that much.

Besides, I didn't even know the guy. For all I knew he could very well have been working with who, or what, was creating all this birthday havoc.

I quickly crept down the hall and poked my head into my room. It had definitely been rummaged through, but it wasn't as bad as the rest of the house.

All clear.

I nudged the door of the bathroom open, only to see a few towels thrown around.

Clear too.

That meant the only room left to check upstairs was Jade's room. I gulped nervously at the thought but pushed myself to move towards it anyway.

"Jade? Are you in there?" I whispered through the small crack that the door left ajar.

No answer.

I pressed my eye up against it and tried to get a glimpse of what was inside.

"If you're going to go in, go in. Don't do things halfway." Apollo annoyedly shoved me into the room.

My body collided with the door harshly and it flung open, slamming loudly into the wall behind it.

A disembodied scream emerged from my mouth, I barely recognized that it was me who was screaming. I was so entranced by the massacre that lay inside of it. The walls were streaked with blood, in some places it was so thick that I would have sworn that it was paint. A horrifying smell assaulted my nostrils and immediately my body heaved.

"I swear if you throw up that's the last straw. I'm telling the temple that I never found you."

I was getting sick of his commentary really fast. The only thing that made me truly want to throw up was his misogynistic, egotistical words.

I clenched my fists tightly and held my anger inside. I was tempted to take a swing at his big blueberry looking head, but I had no doubt that his reflexes were faster than mine and I didn't particularly feel like being sliced in two.

"Where is that smell coming from?" I managed to get the words out before having to stifle another gag.

I peeked under the bed.

Nothing.

Checked all of the drawers in her ridiculously large dresser.

Nothing.

The closer I made it to the closet the stronger the smell was.

Oh god.

My hands trembled as I reached for the doorknobs. Whatever was behind there I said a silent prayer that it wasn't Jade.

Pull them open. Just do it. Fast, like ripping a bandaid off. I stood frozen in front of it, trying to gather up the courage to go through with it.

Apollo's sword dematerialized and turned into a stream of water that he guided back into his water pouch.

"Just get it done already!" He nudged me out of the way and pulled the doors open quickly.

Out tumbled the charred remains of something large. It took me a few seconds to fully realize the horror of what it was.

A body.

"What the hell!" I stumbled back into my back pressed up against the sticky wall. I didn't even care anymore.

Apollo crouched down to examine it before nudging it with his foot. Pieces of the carcass crumbled at his touch.

"Oh my god. Oh my god. Oh my god." I hyperventilated. The faster I breathed the faster the room spun in circles. "Please tell me that's not her. That can't be her. I can't handle it."

"First off, right now is not the time for a mental breakdown, so pull yourself together." His words stung like salt poured in an already gaping wound. "Second of all judging by the size and weight I'm guessing that this is a guy. Did she have a boyfriend? Or a brother or someone that would have been here at the house with her?"

I deciphered that whoever Apollo was, he had to be a psycho, or a serial killer or something. Who else could see a body like that and not even bat an eye?

Jade was right. I definitely shouldn't have even trusted him to make it that far with me.

"She had a fiance." Tears streamed down my face. "He went everywhere with her. They were practically inseparable. They were even going to get a place of their own soon, maybe start a family. They had plans, and now they're all ruined." The tears streamed down my face in sobs so violent that my entire body shook.

"Spare me the sob story." He said coldly.

I looked up at him angrily. I couldn't understand how one person could be so utterly heartless and cold.

I tightened my grip around my baseball bat and toted it over my shoulder. "That means that Jade's still out there, right?"

"Are you asking me, or telling me?"

"I'm telling you that I need to find my friend, and you need to leave." I raised the bat threateningly, proud of myself for finally letting a sliver of my true thoughts slip out of my mouth. It was emotionally exhausting to let my guard down enough to let it squeak out under my anxiety radar, but it felt freeing- until he started to laugh.

"What's so funny?" I asked through gritted teeth. I hated that I could feel my cheeks getting red again and my eyes welling up with more tears.

"The fact that you think you have a choice on whether you come with me or not." Apollo said.

In the distance the sound of police sirens headed in our direction.

"Well, we'll see what the police have to say about that." I bolted toward the door but Apollo pulled his water from his pouch, made it into a lasso, and flung it around my feet sending me spiraling to the floor.

I wiggled and screamed, filled with a sudden rage that flowed through me like a river. Something inside me shifted, maybe even broke. And I felt all the anger, and hurt, and disappointment that I'd felt throughout the years explode inside me like a bomb, coming out in the form of my scream. Suddenly the room started to vibrate. It was a low rumble at first until it quickly spiraled into a violent quake. The windows shattered and pieces of the ceiling spiraled to the floor crashing loudly.

There was a sharp pain in my thigh and I looked down just in time to see a tranquilizer dart lodged inside of it before everything turned black.

Chapter 6

My eyes fluttered lightly beneath my eyelids as I roused from my sleep.

"What the hell." I groaned, rubbing at my forehead with the palm of my hand. I'd hoped that it would have at least done something for the pain that seared inside my skull, but no luck.

Around me my fingertips found the soft plush comfort of a blanket. I opened my eyes and stared up at a soft cream colored ceiling, immediately gravitating to the rose embellishment that lined around it.

"Thank gods you're awake. I was starting to think that I should have read the label on the tranquilizer dart before I stabbed you with it." Apollo's voice came from the plush armchair in the corner. "It said it was for small animals, so I assumed it was safe for you too."

My face contorted into a look of disgust and annoyance.

"Where the heck are we?" I glanced around the small room.

It was quaint, and decorated with vintage things. There was a large window beside the bed I laid in, with a series of potted plants in the window all reaching from the depths of their soil begging for the sunlight that it provided.

Even the bed I laid in had a vintage metal frame.

It reminded me of every bed and breakfast that I ever saw in movies.

It was cute and cozy.

It would have been even better without Apollo sitting in the corner staring at me intensely.

"We're at the Eden Manor." Apollo answered.

I raised a brow at the name. It felt odd hearing mine paired with the word *manor* like some rich kid who'd been gifted an entire estate by their parents.

"And before you ask, yes. This is all yours."

My head turned in his direction so fast that it aggravated the headache even more and I winced.

"I'm sorry, what?" I chuckled awkwardly. "Look, like I've said before, I think you have the wrong person. I don't know if you're trying to cut corners and just grabbed the first person you found named Eden for namesake or what. But I'm not it."

"I never cut corners." A glint of anger surfaced in Apollo's cold eyes.

Before I could say another word the golden doorknob on the

bedroom door started to jiggle and I sat up straight, not knowing what the hell was going to walk through the door next or if they were going to try to kill me too.

The door slowly creaked open and my jaw dropped.

Inside walked an apparition of a butler, made completely out of glistening blue water. He was an older man, with hardly any hair, and a butler suit. If it wasn't for the mystical blue tint of his skin he would have been completely see-through.

"What the fuck." I cringed at the words that fell out of my mouth. Swearing was never my thing, I was never comfortable enough in my own skin to feel right uttering the words, but the situation kind of warranted the reaction.

I squinted my eyes. Inside of him little bubbles surfaced and bounced. I felt like I was looking at a man shaped fish tank.

"Hello Miss Eden." He said tenderly.

A man sized fish tank with a British accent. What's next?

"Hi." The word fell from my trembling lips like a deflated balloon, falling flat on the stale energy of the room.

"I'm not sure if you remember me, but I remember you. Water remembers everything, you know." The butler chuckled at his own scientific joke. "I'm Johnathon Matrickle, the proud caretaker of this estate for nearly a century now. Proudly serving the Montgomery family the entire time." He smiled.

I felt a jolt of energy hearing my last name come from his water lips. How many other Eden Montgomerys with a tragic backstory and no parents could there be out there in the world?

"Would you care for a tour of the estate?" Johnathon asked politely.

I stared in awe. My mind was trying to decipher a logical way that any of it could be happening. Maybe I'd finally snapped. Maybe my birthday was my last straw and I was making all of it up in my mind.

A coma. Maybe I'm in a coma.

The thought was random, but it was the most logical reasoning I could think of. I'd read in one of my many books that sometimes comatose patients woke up from extended periods of time and reported that their minds had created alternate realities for them to live in, and they didn't even know they were comatose until they woke up.

The possibility was highly improbable, but so was a butler made completely of magical talking water, so at that point I was willing to grasp on to anything that felt even the slightest bit normal.

"She'd love a tour." Apollo answered for me, quite impatiently actually, but I was in too much shock to care.

I pulled myself from the warm shelter of the covers and realized that my tattered work apron and singed clothes had been changed into some light pink pajamas made out of shimmering silk.

My eyes darted to Apollos, my face bright red.

"Oh don't flatter yourself honey." Apollo snorted. "The maids changed you, not me. The only thing I was concerned with was getting you here in one piece. I didn't give a shit what your clothes looked like."

He's such a freaking charmer.

I racked my brain trying to figure out, if this really was a dream, why the heck my brain would want to torture me with such a character.

Johnathon stood patiently waiting for me to slip the pink slippers on that sat beside the bed.

Everything fit me perfectly, which I had a feeling wasn't a coincidence.

Finally pleased, Johnathon turned around and disappeared in the doorway.

I found myself awkwardly squinting at the ground searching for wet footprints left behind, anything that would prove he was more than a mere figment of my imagination, to no avail.

Apollo scoffed behind me, which urged me to follow through the doorway.

It opened up into a beautifully intricate hallway. The ceilings were high, and beautiful crown molding lined each side. Extravagant portraits graced the walls every so often, with one sitting right beside the doorway. It was of a young man, with bright brown eyes. He sat proudly in a chair and wore an old fashioned suit. My eyes immediately gravitated to a small spot on his forehead, just below the line where his brown hair began to tousle. A scar sat prominently, shaped like a circle with two jagged swirls inside.

I felt like all the air was sucked from my lungs at the sight of it.

"What's that?" I managed to ask, pointing quickly to it.

"That would be the mark of eden. It appears on the firstborn member of each Montgomery bloodline when the carrier magic is transferred from a dying parent." Johnathon answered casually, like all of this wasn't batshit crazy.

I unknowingly rubbed at the spot on the left side of my chest just below my collar bone.

The spot where my identical scar sat.

For my entire life I'd always wondered how the hell I got it. No matter how much research I did, no matter how many situations I thought of I couldn't think of a single thing that would leave a scar as intricate as mine.

I was saddened to say that carrier magic being passed down from a dying parent wasn't even on my list.

"And who is this?"

"That would be Tobias Montgomery. He was a fine man, and an even finer father to yours."

I looked up at the portrait once again. It was hard to believe that the young and vibrant man pictured was my grandfather, someone who was probably long dead.

I nodded my head, deciding to go with the flow. Dream or not

Growing up I'd always wondered what my parents were like. Even more so as their memories faded from my mind. I found myself making stories up about them in my head. They were astronauts who had to send me away so they could go on a trip on the moon. Then they were explorers, setting out to uncharted countries tasked with analyzing the elemental magic that each country held. My personal favorite, though, was that they were spies for the water caste, who were sent on secret missions through the other kingdoms and fought dangerous people which is why they had to send me away to someplace where I could be safe.

This is by far the greatest parent back story yet.

We made our way down the hall and passed by a few more portraits. I quickly noticed that all of them were men, and they all sported the same scar just in different places.

"Why are there no women in the photos?" The question fell from my lips before I even had time to overthink whether or not to ask it.

"Because until you, every heir born to the Montgomery name was a boy. Which meant that every eden was a man. Your parents thought it only fit to name you Eden."

The words rattled around in my mind.

"What do you mean an eden?"

Johnathon held up a hand.

"You'll find out soon enough, but first let me finish the tour Miss Eden."

I clamped my mouth closed and obliged.

Johnathon led us through the halls of the large house. It was bigger than any building I'd ever been in. Even bigger than the nun's boarding school that I was forced to go to as a kid, and back then I thought it was gigantic.

He showed us all the guest rooms, each with a small back story of some distant family member that had lived there in the past. It was a little overwhelming going from an orphan to an heir of an incredibly large, mystically important family, so my brain didn't fully process a lot of what was going on.

But I was assured that I'd over-analyze every single detail before I went to bed like I always do, so I wasn't too concerned.

Johnathon led us down a flight of stairs that brought us to the main floor of the house. That was where it got interesting with weapons rooms, training quarters, and there was even an entire suite dedicated solely to armor.

What the heck kind of things was my family into?

The question plagued my mind. It felt like there was a big piece of the story missing that kept my brain from processing the big picture of why they even owned an estate that big. Why would they have use for so many weapons and armor? And what did that have to do with Jade's disappearance?

We passed by a maid who carried a stack of towels. She smiled politely at me, a look of excitement in her blue eyes.

"How many of you are there?" I asked, only realizing how rude it might have come off after it had already left my mouth.

"I assure you Miss Eden, there is only one me." Johnathon answered coolly. "But if you're referring to people like me, water specters, then there are many in this house. Chambermaids, cooks, servants, there's a whole team and we've been waiting for your arrival. Everyone is quite happy that you're here."

"But where did you come from?"

Johnathon led us through a large sitting room that held two glass doors that led to the back of the manor. Through them I saw a large stone building, hidden by the house and the surrounding woods.

He opened the doors and ushered us through.

"That is a question that I will leave for Mr. Apollo to answer." He smiled at me. "Buckle up, because you're in for a wild ride Miss Eden."

Chapter 7

Apollo and I stood in front of the large stone building. It's architecture was some of the most beautiful that I'd ever laid eyes on, and that was including all the intricate ancient buildings I'd read about in books.

Its stone was a dark grey that sparkled in the direct sunlight. The walls were high and it held a huge stained glass window in the front. It looked more like a Catholic Church in the backyard than anything else.

The stained glass window was the thing that caught my eye most. It stood prominently at the front of the building, and was splashed with vibrant colors that created a scene of all four elements.

What grabbed my attention and refused to let it go, though, was the insignia that was placed in the middle of all four. The circle with two swirls inside of it- just like my scar.

Apollo must have noticed my brow furrow at the sight, because he held the thick wooden door open and ushered me inside the dimly lit building.

"It'll all make sense soon." He said as I passed him.

Inside the building opened up to a square room. As I made my way inside I realized the building felt smaller on the inside than it looked on the outside.

At the front of the dark room sat a shimmering golden chest among an array of burnt out candles and incense. Even in the shadows it seemed to throw off a mystical golden light that drew me in. Before I knew what I was doing I found myself pulled in, walking straight for it.

"What is this?" I asked, tilting my head to one side examining it.

It looked like a treasure chest, perfect and golden. Like something you'd pull right out of a children's book about a pirate adventure. It didn't look like it belonged there among the dark shadows and the dust.

"No one knows. It can't be opened, it's completely sealed. And anyone who tried to break the seal died instantly."

I looked up at Apollo, my eyes wide.

"Mental note, don't touch the pretty chest." I got up from my knees, realizing that there were four rooms that branched off the main one.

Two of them were closed off by slabs of rock, each with a small picture of an element carved into it. Two of the rock slabs hung ajar like giant doors- the fire and the water.

"What is this place?"

"The Temple of Eden." Apollo said. They were the only words that I had ever heard come from his lips that sounded the least bit sacred. He wasn't sarcastic, or rude. He might have even sounded a little amazed, which I got the feeling was a rare thing for him.

I, on the other hand, was never going to get used to hearing my name used in so many different contexts. I wasn't used to anybody saying my name, really at all. Unless it was to ridicule or taunt me.

All of this seemed like a stretch, but my curiosity got the best of me.

"This is where all the sacred texts are that lead to the carriers of each ancient elemental magic." Apollo walked toward the water door and shoved it open enough for both of us to get inside.

Inside was a shrine dedicated to water, even two glowing orbs of water were suspended in the air, the only thing giving the windowless stone room light. Everything was washed in it's cool blue tint.

There were burnt down candles and incense that laid on an altar, and a small treasure chest lay amongst them too. It reminded me of the shimmering golden one, but it looked significantly less magical.

Apollo turned to me with a serious glint in his eye. "Long ago, before the castes were forced to separate by element everyone lived in harmony. Even the elemental magic that ran through everyone's veins was more potent. It was pure, and it was equal."

I followed along with what he was saying, but my mind traveled back to my home in the water caste. I thought about how the magic was disproportionate now, some people could only lift the water stream by stream, others could command the rain.

A world where everything was equal seemed a lot easier.

"Back then there were ancient families that were chosen to lead each caste, and protect the potent magic. They trained their children up to be protectors of the ancient craft as carriers- tasked with passing it on. But over time the magic grew dimmer in some and brighter in others, which led to conflict. People hated feeling lesser, and some even felt threatened. The fire caste, the most chaotic element, fed off of the chaos that ensued and the head fire sorcerer decided that he wanted to keep it that way, so he fed into the flames. Divided the country, and set out to destroy each ancient elemental family that stood in his way."

There was strife woven deep within the blue tones of Apollo's eyes. He was even more serious than usual, probably more serious than any words he'd ever uttered to me since we'd met, but it was hard for me to feed into it. Up until those moments I'd allowed myself to buy into the secret family wealth, the people made of mystical water, I even let myself be open to the death filled treasure chest. But for some reason the story refused to cement in my mind. It seemed far too *out there* for me to grasp. I let him finish his story, but in the back of my mind I began to plot my escape.

I needed to get back to Jade. She was out there somewhere, while I played house.

"The ancient families banded together to combine their types of magic, to bestow a new type of elemental magic on a deserving farm boy. He became the first eden, a mage who can manipulate all four types of elemental magic. The ancient families hid their firstborn children away, in locations so secret that they committed suicide just to ensure no one could find them magically sealed away, and gave only the location to the eden, who in turn saved them here in this temple. But not before they used powerful magic to entrap the fire sorcerer and his family, forced to be frozen for a century."

I nodded nonchalantly, to let him know I was listening.

"Yes yes, but how do you know all of this if the locations were so secret?" I raised a brow, thinking for sure that I'd trapped him with my words- found a loophole that he hadn't thought of.

I was searching desperately for something to disprove everything that I was seeing.

I had fought my entire life to be special. I wished and hoped and prayed that one day I'd know what it felt like to be important, like Jade and Trent and Veronica.

Now that it slapped me right in my face, all I wanted to do was run. Faced with everything I'd ever wished for I wasn't sure if I'd ever really wanted it at all. I would have paid a million dollars to go back to Eden that nobody noticed, free to hide in my bed of anxiety with no one in the world depending on me.

"I know because I'm the water carrier."

His words hit me like a freight train. They were a twist that even I hadn't seen coming, and I make it a point to imagine every possible outcome.

He made his way to the small chest on the altar that hung open, empty.

"Because of the ancient magic woven into the chest, they can only be opened by an eden. And until a year ago I was dormant, hidden behind a mystical waterfall in the middle of the water cast, encased in ice."

"Who woke you up?"

"Your mother."

I stared at him blankly. From what they'd told me, I was the first girl born to the Montgomery bloodline, which meant that if everything he was saying was true my mother had married into this mess.

And if what they said about the scar was true, it meant that my father had died years ago before he transferred his magic to me.

"So how did she open the chest if she wasn't an eden?"

I found myself actually getting into the mystery of it all now. I liked puzzles. My brain loved trying to decipher how the world around me worked and what set of rules it played by.

"You were there, I was hoping you could tell me how the hell it happened."

The look on my face must not have been promising, because Apollo took a step forward closing in the space between us.

There was an electricity that I could feel emanating from his body. Like a spark I could feel.

I looked up at him and he gazed down at me, all brooding and serious.

Behind my eyes there was a spark of magical electricity, like a jolt of energy.

No. No not him.

A startled look came across his face. "Did you feel that too?"

My cheeks burned.

"Oh god it wasn't a spark was it?" His face contorted angrily, shattering every ounce of self esteem I had.

My face must have looked as broken as I felt inside because an immediate look of regret crossed his.

"I didn't mean it like that. There's nothing wrong with you in general. I just- I don't- I can't-"

"I get it!" I yelled a little louder than I'd care to admit. "Just get on with whatever the hell you were going to do."

The outburst scared even me, but I refused to take it back.

That would be my luck. The one moment I was waiting for, all I had left to look forward to and my mate was a total magical douchebag who only cared about saving the world.

I was stupid to think the universe would destroy every aspect of my existence and have enough mercy to leave my love life intact.

That's not how life worked for me. That's never how it had.

Apollo's face went stone cold again and he moved in closer. I would be lying if I said I didn't feel a new sense of attraction to him that wasn't there before the spark, but I'd never admit it. I found myself noticing new subtle nuances about him that I hadn't before, like how he clenches his jaw sharper when he concentrates. I noticed his presence more as he closed in the space between us, and for the first time ever I found myself wanting him in ways I'd never wanted someone before, and I hated it.

This is not how it was supposed to happen. I gripped in my mind.

But still I couldn't help but marvel at his broodingly handsome good looks. It was like something inside my mind switched on like a magnet and it was pulling me to him. I wondered if he felt it too, although his frozen features would never let on. He'd never tell.

"I need you to hold still, this is going to hurt. How much, I don't know. I've never done it before myself, but I've seen it done." He reached his hands out to touch my face but I dodged his grip.

"Wait just a minute, that's not the kind of thing you tell someone before you open up to them about their magical back story, reveal your own, and freaking find out that you're their fated mate."

Apollo rolled his eyes. "Quit stalling. You're just wasting time."

His hands found my hips and pulled me back into him, my body pressing up against his.

It was probably unintentional, but he awoke an aching between my legs that I hadn't felt before. One that begged for him and only him.

"What is it that we're doing?" I asked, my voice quieter now.

"We're going inside our heads."

Chapter 8

Apollo's fingertips graced the smooth skin of my cheeks and I caught myself shivering beneath his touch. It wasn't entirely because I'd never been touched that closely by someone I felt such a ferocious attraction too, his ominous warnings of pain had a lot to do with it.

You can't just tell someone something's going to hurt with absolutely no context.

Apollo closed his eyes and concentrated, and I stared back at him waiting for the imminent pain.

The next few seconds ticked by so slowly that I could have sworn they were minutes. The silence of the temple rested so thick that I was almost afraid to utter a single word, but I had to.

"I don't think this is working." I whispered for unknown reasons.

Apollo's eyes opened laced with confusion.

"I don't understand. It's supposed to be. I should be able to use the water in your body to pull the memories from your mind"

"Right." I drew the word out longer than I'd meant to, adding a hint of skepticism.

I decided that I was finished entertaining the notions. Inside I still held doubts on the reality of the place. There was a possibility it could all have been a dream, or a hallucination, maybe I hit my head too hard in the blast of the coffee shop. But either way I had to at least try to find Jade.

"I need some time." I nearly stuttered as the words came pouring out.

Apollo's icy blue eyes met mine and I squirmed underneath his sights.

"To think about all of it, not the whole fated mates thing." I tripped over my words, digging myself deeper into a hole.

Apollo rolled his eyes. "We're not fated mates. Carriers can't have mates. Their sole purpose is to perfect their elemental magic. A mate would only distract from that."

I couldn't tell if it was me he was trying to convince, or himself. Either way I pushed my hurt feelings aside and pushed through the heavy wooden door of the temple.

The air was brisk and fresh compared to the stale air inside of it, and I felt like I could finally breathe.

I didn't hear Apollo try to follow or chase after me. I assumed he was still in the temple trying to convince himself that it wasn't a spark that we had felt. It didn't matter, though, by the time he worked through whatever emotional baggage made him come off as such a dick, I would be long gone. I'd make sure of it.

I walked around the front of the manor and sighed a breath of relief to see a small car parked in the circular driveway. I had been hoping that we made it here by actual transportation and not by some weird magical form.

A car was easy to hijack, magical teleportation? Not so much.

I glanced around the front yard quickly, searching for any prying water filled eyes, but found nothing, so quickly I made my way to the black car. I slipped into the driver's seat and rummaged for a set of keys.

"Come on. Come on." I mumbled to myself, like that would make them appear faster.

I dropped the glovebox down and a map tumbled out making a new home on the car floor. It's absence revealed something that grabbed my attention- a small black handgun. Just the sight of the weapon gave me an uneasy feeling so I scrambled to pick the map up to shove back into the glovebox.

That was before I noticed the markings on it, and the bright red circle around my house. A strange sense of violated privacy bubbled up inside me but I shook it off, deciding to keep the map out instead. Their creepy loss was my gain. I had everything I needed to make it home now, I just needed the freaking keys.

Finally I pulled the sun visor down and they tumbled into my lap with a small tink.

A smile spread across my lips as I slid them into the ignition and right before I was about to turn them a knock came from the drivers side window.

I turned to see Johnathon's wispy blue figure standing politely beside the car. He was nearly see-through in the sunlight.

I fought with myself for a second. Speed off rudely, or hear him out.

Ugh, Eden, why are you like this? I scolded myself, a sense of urgency crept up.

I knew with every second that passed Apollo was probably closer to realizing something was up. And while I doubted that Johnathon could or would stop me, I had no doubt that Apollo would drag me from the car. He'd probably even go as far as to lock me in the manor like a lost princess until I promised to behave and be his magical savior.

No thank you. Being Jade's savior was enough responsibility for me.

"Hi." I said with an awkwardly polite smile as I rolled the window down.

"Hello Miss Eden. I was simply wondering if we should expect you back for dinner." His accent was thick and melodic.

"Well, Johnathon," I sighed. "I don't know. I have a friend that's in a lot of trouble. And right now I'm the only person who knows it. She's like a sister to me, the only family I have. So I have to go."

Johnathon nodded understandingly. "Well, maybe one day

you'll come to the understanding that we're your family too." He said with a smile. "Drive safe now."

With that he turned and slinked back into the manor without another word.

I watched him in the rearview mirror until his blue figure disappeared. Although his words sounded cheery I could tell there was a twinge of sadness behind them, and if there was one thing I hated it was letting people down.

But Jade was a person, and I couldn't stomach the thought of letting her down more.

So I twisted the key and the car hummed to a start.

"Hold on Jade," I took a final look at the map and threw the car in drive. It slowly lurched forward and I pulled out of the driveway. "I'm coming."

***

I was surprised at how fast the drive seemed to go. The manor wasn't very far from my home near the outskirts of the water caste. I knew I was getting close when I started to see more dams and the trusted water powered energy plant.

Each caste used its own element to power its region. The fire cast used heat energy, the air caste used wind energy, even the earth caste used the power of solar energy. Ours was water. Everything, all the way down to the internet, was powered by the water power plants. I'd lived right around the corner from the region's main plant for most of my life, whether it was in Jade's house or the academy. I always knew when it came into view I was almost home.

My mind wandered as I drove about what I might come home to. Maybe Jade had found her way back and she was waiting for me. Maybe this was all an elaborate birthday prank, god knows when you have money you can afford to pull anything off. Buying an entire abandoned manor and enlisting the help of special effects actors to prank your friend on her birthday? That sounded up Jade's alley. She was extra like that, and had money basically coming out of her ears. What else was she going to do with it?

I got lost in my thoughts like I often did as my brain tried to come up with every possible outcome of what I might run into when I got home. It went into overdrive trying to prepare me. So much so that I nearly missed the street I was supposed to turn on.

Come on Eden. Get your head in the game. I parked a few blocks away from our house, just in case we needed to make a get away, or someone was watching the house. I didn't want to tell on myself before I even got there.

Something in the pit of my stomach churned into an uneasy gurgling mess whenever I thought about going through the front door. The feeling went so much deeper than a nagging anxiety, it was intuition. It was so real and so intense that I was afraid what it would morph into if I went against its wishes and used the front entrance anyway, so I rerouted myself to go through the back yard.

It was pretty early in the morning and the streets of the city were dead. Once again I found myself making my way through the brisk dew filled morning air. I'd guessed that Apollo's tranquilizer was stronger than he'd anticipated and I'd slept through the entire day before- slept my birthday away in a strange place.

A twinge of doubt about whether that would be part of any prank Jade pulled swept through me, but I tried to dismiss it. There were weirder things in the world than my best friend pulling off a semi-cruel birthday heist.

I wanted so desperately to believe it, that I just did.

A small puff of frozen air traveled from my lips as it mixed with the even colder outside air before turning to smoke and trailing into the sky. I turned down an alley that separated the backyard of houses on two different streets and my house came into view. It looked so still and peaceful in the early morning light. The world around me was so quiet that if I forgot about the last twenty-four hours I could almost convince myself that everything was alright again. Everything was normal. I would open the back door, creep upstairs, and find Jade passed out in her lush pink bed, probably surrounded by takeout with her TV still playing in the background.

I could almost see it in my mind, and it was a comforting feeling. A small illusion of normalcy in a world that no longer made sense to me.

It was easy to spot my house amongst the rest because it was the only back yard that had a white metal fence encasing it.

Jade was serious about her privacy.

I crept up to it, and flipped open the keypad that was attached to the security system. I knew the key code by heart, so bypassing it was the furthest worry from my mind as I slipped inside the yard and crept up to the rear porch.

I tried to peek in through the small window that led to the kitchen, but it was too dirty.

Another thing I constantly begged Jade to clean because I was sick of doing it myself all the time.

On to the list of complaints.

I shoved the thought aside knowing good and well I was never going to bring it up to her.

After the entire shit show was over I'd just clean it myself. I didn't waste time lying to myself by saying otherwise.

I made my way to the small white keypad beside the back door, and noticed it was scorched to the point where the circuits were fried. There was no day I could press a single melted button, let alone disarm the security system.

I held my breath and turned the doorknob, hoping that the entire system was fried. It wasn't anything money couldn't fix, and Jade had enough of it.

The back door slowly opened and I gnawed on my inner cheek, waiting for the thirty second grace period to pass on pins and needles.

Nothing.

No sirens sounded, no alarm went off, which meant that our whole system was shot. I made my way through the kitchen and up the stairs, strategically walking around the sharp shards of glass. The house was still trashed, so I hadn't made that up in mind. But it was time for the actual moment of truth.

I nudged Jade's bedroom door open with my foot and my heart sank.

The room was still splattered with blood. On the floor in front of the closet where the charred body once sat now sat an outline of tape. And an X of police tape covered the door.

Jade was nowhere in sight.

I tore the police tape down and walked inside. Everything was still overturned, and the reality set in.

This wasn't a prank. It wasn't a dream, or a hallucination, it was all real. Terribly and horribly real.

My necklace. I suddenly remembered the trinket that had been hanging around my neck when I was dumped on the steps of the reformatory. I rushed to my bedroom down the hall. I stepped over the overturned mattress and ignored all the clothes ripped from the dresser.

Whoever was here was looking for something. I had a feeling I knew what it was.

I made my way to an old framed poster that clung to the wall above my bed and pulled it down revealing a hole in the wall. I'd decided to turn lemons into lemonade long ago and use it as a hiding space after Jade had very obviously claimed the room without the defect.

I reached inside and pulled the small locket necklace from it. I could never get the locket open, but I still wore it my entire childhood. I told myself that as long as I wore it I'd be close to my birth parents, and maybe they could find me still.

After I'd given up and my hope turned to a slow burning resentment towards them years ago it found a new home in the crook in the wall.

I slid it around my neck and replaced the framed poster in front of it, like that would help make up for the disaster that was the rest of the house.

It was a small act, but it made me feel safe amidst the chaos.

It was something I could control.

I climbed down from the bare bed frame and made my way back into the hallway before I stopped, frozen in my place.

My heart jumped from my chest as I was met by an entire SWAT team, waiting in the hallway.

"Drop your weapon and put your hands where I can see them!" The man in the front yelled from behind his tactical mask.

I looked over at the handgun before dropping it.

I knew it was a stupid idea to even grab it in the first place, but I didn't know what I was walking into.

"This is all a misunderstanding guys." I said amidst a nervous laugh as an array of red dots from the sights of their weapons splashed across my chest.

One wrong move, a single muscle twitch even, and I knew I was toast.

Then no one would get to the bottom of where Jade was.

An officer rushed over to me and threw handcuffs around my wrists behind my back.

"Eden Montgomery, you're under arrest for the murder of Charles St. John." He said as he drug me down the crooked stairs.

Crap

Chapter 9

I'd never been in trouble before- with the law that was. Even growing up in the academy when all the other kids wanted to go out and toilet paper houses or play ding dong ditch using their water magic, to mystically knock on doors and watch in dismay as people opened them and got sprayed in the face- I stayed behind.

I already felt inadequate among everyone else, I didn't want to feel like a criminal too.

But there I was, being stuffed in the back of a police car as reporters lined the sidewalks and my neighbors looked on with horror spread across their faces.

It pulled out a twinge of anger in me. None of them even knew who I was before the crap show erupted, yet they lined the sidewalks now ready to defame me at the first chance they got- cellphones held high

Before the officer closed the door a reporter's question made its way to me.

"Is it true that you killed your best friend and hid her body, only to set her fiancé on fire and flee the scene?"

The question made my stomach ache, and my skin crawl.

Is that really what they think I did? Is that why no one is out there looking for Jade?

The door slammed abruptly in my face and the police sirens at the top of the car sounded loudly. I watched as the scenery passed by, slowly at first before it gradually morphed into an indecipherable blur.

I hated the feeling that rested in the pit of my stomach. It was a mix of my usual sadness, I was comfortable in that. But it was the anger that was unsettling. I wasn't an angry person, not by a long shot.

But it bubbled inside of me, simmering slowly and I was afraid I was about to burst. I didn't know what would happen after that.

I couldn't stop going over every detail of my humiliation on repeat. Being dragged from my home in handcuffs and accused of murder when I went out of my way for my entire life to make sure I didn't disrupt a single fly.

I bent over backward to try to make myself invisible, and I couldn't believe where it had gotten me.

The scalding anger stirred inside me, simmering the entire drive to the station.

***

An officer shoved me into a cold metal chair in a bleak interrogation room, with complete disregard for my comfort.

I glared up at him with the weight of all the words I wanted to say but didn't dancing on my tongue.

Somehow the air inside the small cement room felt even colder than the brisk air outside, and it sent a shiver up my spine.

The officers left me alone, with nothing but a glass of water perched on the shiny metal table and my thoughts.

My eyes immediately darted to the large window against the back wall. I'd watched enough movies to know that it was a two way mirror. There was probably a room full of psychiatrists on the other side happily waiting to diagnose me, declare me insane, or simply find a way to pin the whole thing on me.

There was no use in demanding a phone call, the only person I had to call was missing. There was no use demanding a lawyer either, because I didn't have the funds. Even if I did, I was sure that they would have thought I was guilty too. Who would believe me if I said I was actually a long lost powerful mage who thought that she didn't have any magic, but turned out she had all types? And she was now running from a mysterious fire mage who happened to burn her best friend's fiancé to a crisp and may or may not have her in his possession?

Nobody.

I knew I barely even believed it, and I was living it.

My thoughts trailed back to the manor and Apollo. Maybe I was safer there-stupid to leave.

But in my defense, I was on the verge of an identity crisis and just found out a lot of magical shit that would be hard for anyone to swallow.

The door to the interrogation room swung open and two somber looking cops pranced their way inside. They looked nearly identical, both hitting the stereotypical cop image precisely, beer bellies and all.

I could tell right away by the smile on one's face, and the scowl on the other that they were about to hit me with good cop-bad cop. Like I was an idiot that had never watched a single television show in my life.

The smiling one looked nice enough, round face, red cheeks, grey hair. He looked like the type of person that would play Santa Claus in one of the vintage movies I loved to watch, back when Christmas was still a celebrated holiday.

The other guy's round face had harsher features, and his thick brows furrowed over his cold eyes.

I could tell that he was the type of person that liked playing the bad cop.

"I'm Officer Smith, and this is Officer Johnson." The bad cop said.

He pulled out a metal chair from the spot across from me and it creaked beneath his weight. Officer Johnson did the same, sitting quietly beside him.

"Hi, I'm Officer Johnson." He held out a hand to shake mine.

I had it all planned out in my head. I was going to be angry. I was going to refuse to talk- really make them realize that they had the wrong person and I was pissed about it.

But Officer Johnson held his hand out across the table waiting for a handshake and I caved, just like I did every other time I planned a big stand for myself in my head.

I couldn't let people down, and that was my downfall.

I forced a smirk as I grabbed his hand.

"Eden."

"Well, it's nice to meet you Eden. Although, I wish it was under better pretenses."

I simply gave him a nod and watched him unload the small briefcase he was holding, spreading manilla folders across the table.

I made the mistake of glancing up at Officer Smith, meeting his angry cold glare.

My eyes quickly darted back to the table and I felt my cheeks warm with embarrassment.

The familiar ache of anger nibbled at my stomach, this time at myself.

I hated that I gave other people the power to make me feel like that. I gave other people the key to my happiness, and in a way that was what had brought me to the jail.

I clenched my fists, trying my hardest to convert the anger into something else- anything I could manage.

Officer Johnson flipped open the first manilla folder, and paperclipped inside was a photo of the coffee shop on its opening day. The building was pristine, and outside of it stood Jade with a huge pair of scissors, ready to cut the opening day ribbon. Even from the outside glimmers of the hot pink interior shone through the windows.

Johnson tapped a solid round finger against the photo solidly.

"You work here, correct?"

"Yes, I did." I said, careful not to trip over my own tongue. I refused to give them any more reason to assume my guilt.

"Before you burned the place down." Smith said from across the table. He didn't even bother adding a question mark to the end of his statement. In his eyes I was already guilty.

"Excuse my partner here, he's a little cranky." Johnson said, to which Smith added an eye roll. "What he meant to ask was, if you were there on the day that it burned down?"

Both of their eyes burned into my skin, and I could feel my chest heave under the weight of their gaze- not to mention however many people there were behind the glass. It was like I could feel them all watching me, judging my every move.

My chest felt tight, and my face grew warmer with every passing second. If I didn't know better I would have sworn the room was creeping in on me. My heart thudded fast and loud in my chest.

They could hear it. I swore they could. Everyone could.

They knew, they had to, and my first instinct?

Lie.

"No." The word came out of my mouth too quickly, nearly falling into a jumbled mess on the table in front of me. "No, it was my birthday. So I slept in."

Anxiety danced across my skin like a band of needles.

Johnson nodded and an exhausted look crossed his face.

"And that's your final answer?"

I nodded, cheeks ablaze.

Johnson sighed, picked up his briefcase, and pushed himself to stand. "Then this is the end of the line for me, kid. I'm sorry that you didn't respect me enough to tell the truth."

His words stung my perfectionist, people pleasing soul and the heavy metal door slammed behind him.

My eyes snapped back to Smith, who had a smirk on his face. Somehow he even managed to make his smirk feel any, defying all laws of physics to do so.

His eyes burned holes twice as hot into my skin, like hot pokers.

"See that? That was the first shovel of dirt you dug down into your own grave. The next few words that come out of your mouth will determine how deep you go. You're going down either way, but you get to decide how far." His words were almost as smug as the look on his face.

He reached over and pulled the photo of the coffee shop from the paperclip it sat beneath, revealing another, more recent, photo beneath it. It showed the shop black and smoldering.

My heart wrenched at the sight, the trauma of the day rushing back to me over the walls I'd built to contain it.

My eyes threatened tears but I blinked them back ferociously.

If that wasn't enough, he pulled that photo back to reveal a final one.

A space on the charred ground, left untouched by the soot. It was in the perfect form of a person, like a puzzle piece missing from a nearly completed puzzle. It was the spot where I woke up from the blast.

Not a single inch of the floor that was beneath me was touched by the flames. A phenomenon that even I couldn't explain to myself, short of Apollo's ramblings of the tale of eden.

"Any of this ringing a bell?" He unfurrowed his brow momentarily to raise it at me.

"Not at all." The words tasted sour coming out of my mouth. Lying wasn't something I did. It wasn't something I was used to but I knew once I started I needed to tell more, otherwise the web would come undone- and I would too.

Smith sighed, pulled another file from the tabletop and opened it up revealing the photo inside.

Crap.

A photo of my cell phone, unscorched by any flames stared up at me. A key piece of evidence that I didn't think I could explain away with lies.

"Does that look familiar Eden?"

I swallowed hard, and forced myself to nod.

"Yes. It's my cellphone. I was looking for it all morning. I must have left it there the night before."

"And how do you explain the call to the station that was placed on it seconds after the explosion?"

A wave of anxiety swept through me.

Crap. I forgot about that. My thoughts were so jumbled in my head from Apollo, and the manor, and everything all at once. Tripping up wasn't like me. Lying wasn't like me either, but I knew if I ever did I would carefully analyze all the factors. Overthinking was my thing.

But I'd missed an important part of the puzzle, and now they had me right where they wanted me.

Officer Smith's lips curled ever so slightly at the edges at the sight of me squirming under the mess I'd created for myself. I'd started out simply trying to keep them from assuming my guilt, but ended up driving the nails into my own coffin instead.

I didn't know what to do, or where to go, but I needed time. Time to think without the constant gaze of everyone here.

"I want a lawyer." The words tumbled from my lips before I even had time to think about them.

Chapter 10

The smirk was immediately wiped from the officers face with the words. It went cold, and emotionless.

"Now listen here you little punk. Once those words come from your lips I can't help you anymore."

"Is that what you were doing?" I snapped, looking him directly in the eyes.

The anger simmered inside of me, reminding me that it was there.

Smith's face turned red at the comment. He was about to blow a gasket, it was easy to see, just like all the other bad cops who lost their cool.

He opened his mouth, ready to strategically rip me to shreds with his words, when a small knock came from behind the mirror.

He was being summoned.

His mouth clamped tightly, but the anger was still ablaze in his eyes. He grabbed my cuffs, tightened them around my wrists, and fastened them to the table- the cherry on top of his anger sundae.

He took one last look at me and huffed before disappearing through the door.

I huffed back angrily grunting, but only after I was sure the door was completely closed.

I was stuck in an impossible situation.

The room grew quiet, and I was left with nothing but my thoughts. I knew what happened next. They had to make calls, get me a public defender, and they couldn't talk to me until they did. I knew for a fact that there were only a few in the entire water caste, so it would take some time for them to track one down.

Until then it would be just me, alone in the mess I'd made for myself. I caught myself wondering what Apollo was doing. I tried to imagine how angry he must have been when he found out I was gone *and* that I'd hijacked the car.

I wondered if he thought about following me, or if he had just cut his losses.

My first thought was the latter.

There wasn't anything inherently special about me. From my plain brown hair to my matching brown eyes, nothing about me stood out. Despite his persistent argument that I was an all powerful mage, there was no proof that I even held the power that he thought I did.

If I was him I would have cut my losses. Everyone did when it came to me.

My mind wandered back to my school days, when the nuns drilled it into my head over and over again. It stuck with me everywhere I went, ringing in my ears and ever present in the back of my mind.

Growing up I didn't even wonder why my parents had abandoned me, it was obvious. It wasn't like they were leaving anything special behind.

That mixed with the daunting realization that they were probably going to give me the death penalty, strapped to a chair and thrown into the sea was almost enough to send me into an emotional shut down. Being completely numb to the world sounded like a good deal.

Just when I was about to emotional check out there was a prominent knock on the door. A tall man in an old brown suit scurried inside too quickly for me to see his face. He immediately turned his back to me and made his way to the mirror pulling the blinds over it, sheltering us from prying eyes.

That was awfully fast for a public defender.

I watched curiously, until he turned around and I froze.

The red hair, the sharp jaw kissed by a trim red beard, the scar that ran through his left eye, it all stopped my heart and made time freeze.

It was him. The mystery guy from the coffee shop. The guy that was there when everything went down.

I must have looked as stupid and shocked as I felt because his lips curled into a smirk too.

He wore a phony pair of glasses, and had his hair slicked back enough to pass as professional.

He pulled out the rickety metal chair and it's squeal pierced through the air, waking me from my semi trance- jolting me back to reality.

He placed his briefcase on the ground beside him and folded his hands on the table in front of him. "Well hello Eden."

His words were smooth. They reminded me of a snake slitting seamlessly in the grass, completely undetected until it's fangs were in your ankle.

There were a million different things I wanted to say, but they all refused to leave my lips.

"My name's Asher Phoenix, and I'm going to be your attorney."

"Bullshit." The words escaped me, but they felt like someone else's. They weren't mine, they belonged to the anger that lived inside of me.

A half chuckle rolled off Asher's tongue as he pulled the glasses from his face and rested them neatly beside him on the table. Without them it was easier to get a clear look at the emerald green eyes that he hid behind them. They were so pure, and so mischievous it was like they were looking directly into my soul.

"Unfortunately for you I'm also your judge, jury, and executioner."

His words gave me goosebumps.

I pursed my lips tightly, not giving him a single second of the satisfaction of knowing that he was under my skin.

My eyes locked on his, and it felt like the blazing anger that had been resting in the pit of my stomach was clawing its way up my throat, only to rest behind my eyes. He stared into mine with a devious smile that told me he was ready to put an end to me right then and there when I felt a twinge of something in my eyes.

Like a zap of electricity, a lighter being flicked to ignition. A magical feeling that cemented itself into my mind.

His brows pulled together in confusion and he hurried to scoot his chair backward and jump to his feet.

"Wait a minute. You felt that too." I said, in awe. "No, was it a-"

"No." He cut me off, his words stern. He fumbled for his mischievous anger, the one that had once blazed inside him so bright. It was like the spark of magic had completely thrown him off of his mission, off his game. He hadn't been expecting it any more than I had.

"It was. It was a spark, wasn't it."

I didn't mean for the awe to lace my words so thick, but it did.

He tried to avoid my eyes, but couldn't. Ours locked together, and in an instant it was like I just knew that it was. There was no doubt about it, we had sparked, which meant-

"I have no need for a spark. Or a mate. Or anything for that matter." His voice was gruff and angry. "As far as I'm concerned this is no more than one of your magical tricks. I know edens can do things that no one else can." He tried to reason with himself, but his words gave him away.

They caught my attention, and brought me back to the matter

at hand.

"How do you know about the edens?" I snapped.

My mind traveled back to the temple. The two doors that hung open, the water carrier and the fire one.

"You're the fire carrier." I said, more for myself than for him.

His expression didn't waver. The look in his eyes told me that he had found his evil footing once again. He remembered what he came here to do.

"It doesn't matter what I am. All that matters is that in a few minutes this entire building will be burnt to the ground with you inside, and that will be the end of our little eden problem."

With that he slid his glasses back on and straightened his tie. He opened the heavy metal door and billows of thick black smoke flowed in from the doorway, quickly rising up and pooling at the ceiling. A wave of heat followed it.

He glanced over his shoulder one more time, reluctantly this time. Just to get one last look at me. "I'll tell Jade you said hello." He uttered the words before he snapped his fingers and disappeared out of the doorway.

At the snap of his fingers, the briefcase he had set beside the doorway burst into flames like the wick of a candle touching a mat. It erupted, but it didn't just burn itself. It flames started to spider their way out from the case, and stick to the concrete.

My heart jumped and sunk all at the same time. It was official. I knew who had Jade.

I had never felt such a vivid mix of relief and fear at the same time. I glanced down at the flames. I was no good to her if I was dead.

They had to be something mystical. There was no way that concrete would catch fire like that.

I pulled on the cuffs that were fastened to the table with no luck. The table was bolted to the ground, and there was no way I had to brute strength to rip it from its anchors.

Meanwhile the flames crept closer and closer. Across the rooms they had already made their way to the opposite side, climbing up the wall like flaming threads of ivy. It was like they were purposely taking longer to get to me, forcing me to watch the entire thing go up in flames, saving me for last like a sick dessert waiting to be devoured.

The air grew hotter by the second, threatening to suck every ounce of moisture from my lungs. The metal table and the metal chair quickly absorbed the heat, and I knew I only had a matter of seconds before they covered me in the agony of burns.

Life was looking bleak. Even more bleak than my life normally was, and that was saying a lot. I closed my eyes, and took a deep breath.

Apollo had said that I held the power to control all four elements. I needed that now more than ever, which meant it was a great time to start believing in myself. There was no better motivator than imminent death creeping up on you and breathing heavily down your neck.

Or maybe that was the heat of the flames.

Either way, I closed my eyes and searched inside myself. As deep down as I could go, finally forced to believe that somewhere in there I held the power that I'd always wanted.

I opened my eyes and stared at the cuffs intently, willing water to come from anywhere, and help me break the chains.

I stared so hard that my eyes started to hurt, when suddenly a long clear stream of water lassoed from across the room and connected with the chains, slicing them clean in half.

My mouth hung open, eyes fixated on my wrists that had been freed from the anchor of the table.

"I did it. I really did it." I said outlaid, a smile crossing my face.

For the first time since this all began I really started to believe that I could be the eden that everyone was looking for. Maybe I did hold the powers of each element inside of me. I could unlock them if I just believed hard enough.

"Oh will you quit playing around and come with me? I don't feel like getting burnt to a crisp today!" Apollo yelled from the other side of the room. He held a stream of water suspended mystically in the air, trailing from the ouch on his side.

My heart sunk into the molten floor once again.

Of course! The one time I actually believe in myself, it isn't actually me. I grumbled in my head.

"Let's go!" Apollo's voice boomed. He was no longer asking, he was demanding.

I hated to admit that it did something to me deep inside, stroked a part of me that I didn't know I liked stroked.

I rushed to the door beside him, and he used his water to create a shimmering shield, held out in front of him. He wrapped his hand around my wrist and held on tightly, dragging me through the flames as he charged forward.

His shield would slowly evaporate, but there was a steady stream of water flowing to it from his pouch. He really came prepared, something I wished I had done.

We made our way down the hall when I heard screams coming from behind a closed break room door.

I planted my feet firmly on the ground, but Apollo just yanked me harder and my feet skated.

"Stop!" I punched him in the shoulder.

He raised a brow at me, but stopped. "That was cute. What? What do you need that is so damn important that we need to stop in the middle of a burning building that I ran into just to save you?" He yelled, and my eyes threatened to spill tears, but I didn't think there was any more liquid in them. I couldn't cry if I wanted to, thanks to the scorching blaze.

"There are people trapped inside there."

"So?" He asked, his face unbothered.

A string tugged at my heart. I couldn't just let people die.

"So, we need to save them."

"You mean I."

"I mean whoever the hell can do it faster so we don't both die."

An impressed look crossed Apollo's eyes.

"Fine."

With that his shield thinned out into a whip made of water again, and he swung it, snapping the handle of the doorknob off. The door flung open and a bunch of people spilled out of it. The two officers who had been interrogating me included.

They were less concerned with me, though, and more concerned with getting somewhere where the air didn't singe every hair on your head.

Apollo assumed his position again, shield in hand, and we raced out of the building leaving the others to fend for themselves.

We burst through the front door and a rush of cool air filled my lungs. The contrast was sharp, and sent me into a coughing fit.

Apollo grabbed me by the arm and pulled me into the back seat of a car waiting nearby. He climbed into the passenger seat and the car started quickly. We sped off just in time to see the officers spilling out of the building right before it collapsed completely.

"It's good to have you back Miss Eden. I trust you found what you were looking for?" Johnathon asked from the front seat.

"I did." I mumbled.

Apollo turned to me, his eyes icy and cold.

"You are the stupidest person I've ever met. I have no idea what you were thinking, or if you had a death wish but either way what you did was selfish there are more people counting on you here than just you or Jade." His words spewed out angrily, and I cowered beneath them.

After years at the academy, being belittled and shamed I couldn't handle the weight of others anger being piled on top of me.

The look in Apollo's eyes shifted as he saw me shrink and he quieted himself.

I blinked back tears and shifted my eyes to the window.

"But I'm glad you're okay." He sighed and my eyes darted back to his.

Something inside them changed, they were softer, less cold.

"Please don't do that again, okay?" He asked. His voice was laced with sadness now.

"Okay."

Chapter 11

The entire ride home I couldn't get Asher's face out of my mind. Every time I closed my eyes I saw it, feeling the spark over and over again.

I didn't understand it. The rules were, you could only spark with one person. Everyone knew it.

So how had I sparked with Apollo *and* Asher.

And also, why was the universe such a sarcastic bitch?

I was upset that I'd sparked with one ornery, egotistical guy so it threw another in the midst.

One that kidnapped my best friend no less.

My mind wandered back to his words, and the look in his eyes as he said it. There wasn't a trace of remorse in sight.

But there had been after the spark. It was there for only a second, not long enough for anyone else to even register- but I had.

Up ahead the driveway came into view, but the manor was nowhere to be found. Where the building should have stood, sat an empty field.

"Where's the manor?" I wondered if I had gotten mixed up.

"Oh it's there, just wait." Johnathon said, with a hint of excitement in his normally monotonous tone.

We turned into the driveway and our car passed through a strange rainbow haze, like the spray from a hose when the sunlight reflects off of it, leaving vibrant colors in its path.

As soon as we got to the other side the manor appeared, in it's white elegance. A few hours ago when I busted out, I never expected that I'd be back so soon, and excited to see it at that.

"It's a mirage cast." Apollo explained. "It was set by the edens a long time ago, it uses small amounts of water vapor in the air and the humidity to bend and shape the light, making others see what we want them to- nothing."

I sat in the back seat dumbfounded. I had no idea that water magic could even do anything that complex.

"And when it needs to, it can become a barrier, only allowing inside those the magic deems worthy." Johnathon added.

I crawled out of the car and rubbed at my aching wrists. The cuffs had rubbed them raw, and even a few smears of red blood showed.

Apollo's blue eyes landed on them and he sighed.

"Come inside. We'll fix you up."

"I'm fine." I said, too quickly to even consider his proposal.

"No really, come inside." He insisted.

"You know I don't need you to save me all the time." I protested.

"Well you could have fooled me." He grabbed me by the arm and basically pulled me into the house, plopping me down in the large armchair in the sitting room. "You know, for someone so anxious you're also *really* fucking bossy." He grumbled to himself as he rummaged through a large armoire across the room.

"That makes two of us." I mumbled underneath my breath. "I don't consent to this. You can't force me to let you help." I said a little louder. My cheeks warmed at the words.

"Shut up and sit still." Apollo said firmly as he knelt beside me.

He opened a small chest that he had pulled from the cabinet, revealing an array of medical supplies. He soaked a cloth in some antiseptic before dabbing it at the wounds on my wrists. I gritted my teeth at the pain and recoiled, but he tightened his grip on my arm and pulled it back to his body.

He looked up at me, his icy blue eyes exhausted and sighed. "Can you please just let me do this." It wasn't a question, it was an exhausted command.

To be honest I was tired too. Being arrested, kidnapped, and almost murdered takes a lot out of you.

"I'm trying to help you. You know it's okay to let people do that sometimes." He muttered underneath his breath and returned to the wounds on my wrists.

He cleaned them, applied some salve for the slight burns, and wrapped them both tightly for me.

I watched as he worked so diligently and gently- his rough hands sure to hold my small wrists with care. Up until that moment I didn't even know if he knew what the word gentle meant, but it was clear that there was a softer side to him, one that he tried to hide beneath layers of anger and angst.

I watched as he wrapped my final wrist just tight enough to apply pressure to the wounds without hurting them.

He looked up at me and I looked down at him, completely silent. His eyes did all the talking.

Inside me something awakened at the sight of him kneeling in front of me. He was so powerful, so strong, so angry, but he knelt with tenderness in his eyes.

For me.

I hadn't felt a pull to someone like that before. One that came from the inside, and had absolutely nothing to do with how they looked, or acted, or sounded.

In fact I didn't care for most of that about Apollo. Sure he was gorgeous, his blue hair always laid in the perfect wild style, and his jawline did sinful things to me. But he was a dick. He was rude. He was ruthless. He was cold.

Still I felt an ache between my legs for him. I felt an unbelievable calling to consummate the magical spark. To make our fated pairing official, flaws and all.

"That should do it." Apollo stood and put away the medical chest.

"Why didn't you tell me the fire carrier was loose?"

Apollo stopped in his tracks, his back still turned to me.

"He has Jade, you know." I added. "He told me."

Apollo spun around with a new hatred blazing in his eyes. "You talked to him? He's the one that did that to you?" He clenched his jaw and motioned to my wrists. His hands had balled into fists. "Did he hurt you anywhere else, I swear-" His words trailed off on his own.

I looked at him, with my head cocked to the side. I'd never seen him like this, and if I didn't know better I would have sworn Apollo was being territorial, maybe even borderline protective.

But that couldn't be.

I didn't dare mention that I thought Asher and I had sparked too. Not yet.

"Why didn't you tell me he was awake too?" My words coaxed him back to reality.

He took a breath and simmered his anger, unclenching his fists.

"Because I didn't want to believe it." He finally sighed, plopping himself down onto the very expensive looking vintage sofa that sat beside my chair. "The fires, everything. I wanted to believe it was someone else. I told your mother not to, and she promised she wouldn't. But she died with his scrolls and her body was too-" He hesitated looking up at me, gauging my reactions. "Too burnt to tell if she still had them or not."

His words seeped into my soul and I felt a twinge of sadness. I didn't know why. I didn't remember her. I'd even spent most of my childhood hating her, imagining all the nasty things that I told myself I would say when I did find her."

But confirmation that she was not only dead but had also suffered a gruesome end stirred up emotions inside of me that I didn't know I held about the entire situation.

I sat quietly with my thoughts and Apollo let me, gauging my face before continuing.

"Each room in the temple holds the coordinates of each of the original carriers. All of us knew each other before any of this." He gestured around the room. "Before the castes completely alienated one another. Back when things were simpler."

He sighed and there was a look of longing in his eyes. He wanted to go back. And I didn't blame him.

I'd never lived in a time when all the castes were one, but I could imagine. Harmony between them all now seemed impossible.

"There was me the water carrier, Atlas the air carrier, Adler the earth carrier, and Asher the fire carrier."

Someone went crazy with the A's.

"Asher was always a hothead, but he wasn't the sociopath he is today. We were friends once. Best friends."

I didn't have any problem believing that. Both of their pushy passive aggressive attitudes seemed like they would go well with each other.

"But when the castes started to divide the high sorcerer of the fire kingdom- his father- got in his head. He filled it with chaotic magic. Asher fought the hardest when he was sealed away. The fire mages put him somewhere they thought no one would ever look- the heart of a volcano, and that's where I thought he'd stay."

"So if my mother didn't wake him, who did?"

"Someone who obviously wants to reawaken the war between castes." Apollo said. His words rang in my ears.

A war between the castes would be catastrophic for everyone. Each of the elements canceled the others out, it was a way for nature to balance our power I supposed. If the castes were to go into an all out war, there wouldn't be any winner.

And there wouldn't be any survivors either.

I thought about the destruction that had happened at my home in the water caste, and the coffee shop in shambles. The lives that were mercilessly lost, and people who would never get to see their loved ones again. I couldn't handle those small isolated incidents. I couldn't even fathom what it would be like on a countrywide scale. We'd rip ourselves apart.

I couldn't let that happen.

"So what do we do?"

"We use you."

I raised a brow at his wording.

"I mean, you know, we need to awaken your magic."

I laughed. "If I even have any."

Apollo did not look amused. He didn't share in my delight at ripping myself down every chance that I got.

"You do. You just choose not to use it."

His words rubbed me the wrong way. Who the heck was he to tell me about myself?

"I think if I had magic I would have used it by now. Especially when the nuns at my school threw me in a pool every day and watched me drown." I snapped.

Apollo's eyes were wide but I didn't feel a smidge of remorse.

If I had magic I would have used it by then. I wouldn't have let myself down for so many years.

"Okay, chill out." Apollo's voice was stern. "We'll start somewhere else then."

I nodded.

I hadn't meant to get so worked up, but I couldn't help it. There were so many years of pain, and agony that were behind me not being able to control an element. There were so many times that I cried myself to sleep wondering why I was broken. Praying to any god that would listen to bless me with the powers that everyone else used to carefree. I'd spent almost my entire life hating my own existence because of my lack of magical abilities. And Apollo thought he could just swoop in and save me from that too? Like he'd saved me from the cafe fire, saved me from the police station, and I had no doubt would save me from a few more things before the day was through.

I couldn't even think about it. I couldn't let myself believe that the ability had been inside of me the entire time, waiting for me to believe in myself enough. Because that would have meant that for years I already had what I had wanted. And I just let myself down, again.

"So, where do we start?" I asked.

I was new to the whole, saving the world thing.

"Well," Apollo took a minute to think it through. "I guess it's time to go wake up Atlas."

Chapter 12

A pollo had said the words like it was the easiest, most casual thing someone could do. He said them like all we had to do was go upstairs, knock on his bedroom door, and wake him up. But I knew in my stomach that it would be a lot more complicated than that.

Even as I followed him through the backyard and we made our way to the temple my stomach bubbled with anxiety. I had no idea what was coming next, or even what kind of person Atlas was.

If he was anything like Apollo and Asher, I didn't know if I'd be able to handle it. That much angst and testosterone in one place might tear a hole in the space time continuum.

Asher opened the heavy door to the temple and I made my way inside the dark space. Once again my eyes snagged on the shimmering golden chest that sat at the front of the room. It's glisten called to me, stirring awake something deep inside. It was like a magnet that pulled me to it, and next thing I knew I was kneeling in front of it, reaching forward to take hold.

"What are you doing? Trying to get yourself killed." Apollo pulled me back from the chest.

I shook the haze from my mind and turned away from it. "No, I just..." I trailed off and turned my attention to the thick stone slab that held the air symbol. It glowed a bright yellow, almost too bright to even look at. "Did it do that before?" I asked, shielding my eyes.

"Do what?" Apollo shifted his glance from me, to the door, back to me with a look of confusion on his face.

It was apparent by the look on his face that whatever it was I was seeing, wasn't making itself known to him.

Maybe that was part of it.

I looked in the direction of the door and squinted.

The symbol was glowing, but so were four different points on the slab.

I felt the familiar pull inside of me guide me to the door, but this time Apollo didn't stop me. It was like I was on autopilot. I brought my hand to the door in a daze and pressed on the four glowing points of the door. I felt them shift beneath the pressure and click into place like stone buttons. After I pressed each one the light faded into nothingness.

Finally I took the tip of my finger and traced the symbol, erasing the light as I went.

When I reached the end of the symbol the daze lifted, and I

turned to look at Apollo, whose eyes were filled with awe. In front of me the rumble of stone grinding against stone filled the air and vibrated the soles of my feet. I watched as the door slowly pushed itself ajar like the rest of them and a rush of wind escaped from the room.

"It worked." The words tumbled from my lips. "It actually worked." I said, feeling accomplished.

Maybe there was something to this eden stuff after all. Maybe I really did have what it took.

That was a hard maybe.

A soft white glow spilled out from inside, and Apollo and I looked at one another before I took a step inside the small room.

It was a small space, just like the other temple- no bigger than a broom closet. Against the back wall a small treasure chest sat on the shrine, but the candles and incense around this one were lit and burned brightly unlike the ones on the shrine to water. They flickered strongly, as though they had just been lit. Not a drop of melted wax dripped down.

On either side of the shrine two small clouds floated carelessly in the air, suspended by magic. They were mesmerizing to watch, floating like they were sailing on a breeze.

It smelled like fresh air inside, even though there were no windows and I was sure the place had been sealed for over a century.

But I learned that there were things that couldn't be explained, this was one of them.

Apollo followed me inside, our bodies nearly pressing together in the small space. He reached out and was about to pick up the chest when I slapped his hands away.

"What are you trying to get yourself killed?" I said in a mocking voice before a laugh erupted from inside me.

I thought it was funny. Him? Not so much.

The smile slowly faded from my face, tears of laughter still dancing on my waterline. "No, I'm serious." I said. "Do you know for a fact that you can touch the thing without all the instant death that you were talking about?" I turned my head to the side and placed a hand on my hip.

Apollo scowled. He didn't like being bossed around like he bossed everyone else around, and it was so ironic I almost laughed.

"That's what I thought." I said matter of factly. "I'd rather not have you dead because we both know I have no idea what the heck is even going on."

Apollo grunted but he moved out of the way and let me examine the box.

I knelt down, bringing it to eye level, sure not to touch it myself. I didn't even know if I was safe from the warnings of death, and I didn't want to take any chances. Not with Jade out there with that hot headed psycho. I was the only one who knew who she was with, and therefore I was the only one who had a decent shot at saving her.

Getting myself killed by a mystically unknown curse would really put a damper on that plan.

The chest was white, and looked very antique. It had intricate designs and carvings splashed across the entire thing, and in the middle sat a keyhole.

I glanced among the candles and incense that littered the shrine, no key in sight.

I scanned the bare walls, with a million thoughts running through my mind. Was there a trick stone embedded somewhere inside the wall that hid a compartment that held the key? Maybe it was hidden in the floor?

Apollo picked up on what I was thinking about and he started to search the walls, running his fingertips over the rough stone surface.

I thought long and hard, when my eye caught on to one of the clouds that was suspended in the air above the chest. Without thinking I reached out and slipped my hand inside one. It felt wispy and soft like cotton candy. Definitely not what a real cloud would feel like, but I wasn't about to complain.

The cloud was big enough to swallow my whole hand, but there wasn't anything inside it.

I reached out and the second my fingertips slipped into the second cloud it turned dark like a storm cloud. Small flickers of light popped inside of it, like lightning and the cloud quivered like it was a victim of harsh storm gusts of wind.

Inside my fingertips brushed against something smooth and cold.

"Got you." I mumbled as I pulled my hand from the cloud, my fingers wrapped tightly around the white skeleton key.

I had a bad habit of talking to inanimate objects.

"Look at that." Apollo now stood beside me.

In order to look over my shoulder he had to tuck his body in tightly against mine, and it sent a shiver down my spine that pooled in between my legs. He was so close that I could feel his warm breath lapping against the back of my neck.

"If I didn't know better, I'd think you were impressed." My voice was almost a whisper.

"Well do you?"

"What?"

"Know better?" His voice was velvety smooth as it glided to my ears, and I could help but imagine how the lips it came from would feel against my skin- kissing me in as many of my sensitive places he could find.

Pull yourself together Eden! Focus! I pushed my attention back to the key that I held tightly in my grasp.

On one end was a cloud, the other held two prongs that looked like they would fit perfectly in the two holes on the chest.

I took a deep breath and slid the prongs inside. There was a popping noise inside the box and the lock on the outside flopped open, releasing the pressure it held inside.

The box flung open and a mystical white orb flew out so quickly that I didn't have time to relax. It whizzed over our heads and darted out the door leaving only a fading trail of light behind.

"What the hell was that?" I said, finally picking my jaw up off the floor.

"That was Atlas." Apollo said casually. "His consciousness anyway. Now that it was released it will find its way back to his body. It's up to us to find it, and free him. Otherwise he's going to be even more pissed that he's now *conscious* and trapped."

My eyes returned to the chest. Inside all that was left was a small scroll, that was rolled up tightly with a white wax seal holding it closed. The mark on the seal was a cloud, just like the key.

I pulled it from the box, careful not to let my fingertips touch the edges, visions of death still in the back of my mind.

I successfully plucked the scroll from the box and Apollo pulled it from my hands.

I huffed as he broke the seal. Sometimes I wanted to slap him upside the head, but I didn't dare because I knew he could probably kick my ass.

Not that he would, but he could.

And something told me that Apollo Reef was one person who's bad side was one I didn't want to have the honor of gracing.

He unrolled the scroll and looked at it angrily.

"What?" I asked as he tossed it back to me.

"I can't see anything on it." He groaned. "So, do your weird magic thingy or whatever."

"My weird magic thingy." I repeated the words back to him and his cheeks grew red.

"You know what I mean!"

His nerves were rising, it was obvious. But something told me that it wasn't because of the situation or the stakes that were at risk. He was getting unnerved because I could do something he couldn't. Which meant that he actually needed me to complete the mission.

An alpha male like Apollo hated having to depend on someone else, especially someone weaker than him.

And I'd be lying if I said that didn't stroke my ego, even a little. I'd spent my entire life wishing that I was important. Praying for something to set me apart and make me special. I wasn't sure if I wanted the responsibility of being an eden at first, but the way Apollo's eyes looked when he begged me for help made it worth it.

It was the first taste of power over someone that I'd ever gotten in my life and I could see why people went crazy over it. It awoke a hunger for power inside of me that I didn't even know I had. It felt good to be needed, sure, but it felt better to be powerful. To be able to do something that nobody else could, and that was where my true power lay.

I unrolled the scroll and watched as a mystical wind picked up in the small temple. It erupted from nowhere, but it blew strong and brushed over the scroll. As it did ink lines slowly started to sketch on the paper, until it revealed a full map. A bright red X sat in the middle.

"So, where does it say?" Apollo's curiosity was becoming too much for him to handle.

I turned to him, finally feeling a glint of adventure. "Tell me, have you ever climbed a mountain before?"

Chapter 13

I had never been out of the section of the country known as the water caste. If I'm being specific I'd really never had reason to leave my small city in the heart of it either. The Mountain of Aura lay in the outskirts of the air caste, not very far from the manor, but the thought of leaving still shook my stomach in unspeakable ways.

The car hit a bump in the road as Apollo took a sharp right and drove onto a small path that led into the dense forest.

"We're here already?"

"I guess the families decided to keep everyone close to the manor, hidden in plain sight."

The car slowed to a halt at the dead end of the dirt path.

I peered out the window at the dark forest that engulfed us.

The brush from the trees was so thick that barely any sunlight had the chance to fight its way through the vegetation. It was dark, and damp, and something ominous hung over it like a cloud of sadness. I reluctantly pulled myself from the car and took a deep breath.

Even the air felt damp and odd.

I pulled the map from my back pocket and sprawled it out on the car's hood. A bright golden dot appeared on it, shimmering and dancing in the dim light.

"I'm assuming that's us." I laid my finger on it. "Which means we have all this way to go." I traced my fingertip over the parchment, dragging it all the way to the mountain.

That looks like a lot of work.

The truth was, I was exhausted. Being arrested and almost killed drains a girl! The back of my mind was cluttered with thoughts of sleep, and hot baths.

Those were the only things pushing me to keep going. The faster we freed Atlas, the faster I could be back in the manor.

I needed time to rest, recoup, and figure out how the hell I was going to get Jade out of the grasp of Asher. Now that I knew where she was a new fear surfaced inside of me. Was she even alive?

I shivered at the thought, remorseful for even considering a possible reality where she was dead.

"If we move now we could be back by nightfall." Apollo pulled a huge pack onto his back.

The sound of water sloshing came from it.

"Is that *all* water?" I asked.

I had heard of water packs like that, but only for extreme hikers and runners.

"Yeah, I have a feeling that my pouch isn't going to cut it. You never know what you're going to find in this forest. Stay close to me."

Apollo walked off and I trailed closely behind. For a split second his statement sounded more like the plea of a concerned friend, rather than the command of a hard headed frenemy, but I shook it from my head. I was probably making up things that weren't there.

Apollo had made his feelings for me pretty clear- there were none. There was nothing there, there couldn't possibly be.

My mind traveled back to Trent at the coffee house, the gorgeous barista who had humiliated me in front of his girlfriend. I had thought I had a chance then, and look where that got me- absolutely nowhere. I wasn't going to make the same mistake twice. There had to be some other explanation for the spark that we felt.

And Asher.

I couldn't have sparked with two different people, it wasn't possible. I'd never heard of anything like it before.

But I also hadn't heard of a mage who could control all four elements before either.

The further into the forest we got the thicker the darkness grew. Around me all kinds of exotic trees reached into the sky with their twisted branches. They were definitely different from the regular oak and maple that we got in the water caste.

I found myself wondering how they decided who went where

when they split up the country. The fire mages migrated further south for the hotter climates, and the earth mages followed suit. The water mages stayed north, accompanied by the air. Was it strictly based on climate? Or was there more at play to keep the peace?

"So, what was it like?" I found myself asking, breaking the eerie silence that blanketed both the forest and us.

"What was what like?"

"Life before the split? Was it exciting? I couldn't imagine just walking down the street and running into a fire mage, or even earth or air for that matter. This divided society is all I've ever known."

Apollo grunted, as if he were contemplating whether to even entertain my question or not.

I wondered if he would too. He was careful about opening up, and rarely did so. But we were walking into an unknown situation. For all I knew the mountain could be guarded, or booby trapped, or freaking explode the second we got there. This experience really showed me how temporary everything was, and I refused to die with someone I knew absolutely nothing about.

I felt like after the events of the last few days he could at least entertain me, especially on the dreary trudge toward the mountain.

"It was," Apollo paused, searching for the right word. "Exciting. It was diverse. You never knew what you would see walking down the street. At one house you'd see kids having a magical water fight, the next your neighbors would be using their magic to burn the brush in their yard. My favorite was the air mages, though. Instead of cars they opted to use clouds for transportation, there was a highway system in the sky and everything. So every time you looked up you'd see clouds speeding by and you'd wonder where they were going in such a hurry."

He said the words with a smile but his voice was cold and longing.

"Now when I look up I don't see a thing."

His words left a longing inside me too. I'd never experienced it, but it sounded magical.

"You were free to love whoever you wanted to love, fire, air, water, earth, none of it mattered."

"You sound like you're speaking from experience." I said.

A small twinge of pain stabbed at my heart, and I didn't know why. Apollo wasn't mine, and I doubted he'd ever be. But for some reason the thought of him with anyone made my skin crawl.

I shoved the feeling away, stuffing it down deep into the recesses of my being.

"Yeah, I thought I was in love once." The words sounded hesitant leaving his lips. "A fire mage."

"That sounds nice!" I said a little too excitedly, trying to cover up the fact that it didn't sound nice, him with anyone else sounded awful.

"She killed my only brother and tried to kill me too."

"Oh." The words fell flat from my lips followed by silence from us both.

"Well I'm sorry-"

"Shhh." Apollo held up a finger to my lips, brushing against them softly and butterflies fluttered between my legs at his touch.

I didn't even care that it was definitely rude of him to cut me off like that.

I paused, listening for whatever it was that had him so distressed, but all I heard was silence.

"Do you hear that?" He whispered, and somehow his voice managed to get even more enticing.

I raised a brow. It wasn't like I could exactly answer him with his fingertip still pressed against my lips, but I wasn't complaining.

Every time our skin touched it was like something familiar inside of me woke up, even if only for a few pleasurable seconds.

"Exactly" He whispered. "Nothing. Even the birds stopped chirping."

As he said it I noticed it too. The normal sounds of nature had gone missing.

But what did that mean?

"We're getting close. Stay close to me, okay?" Apollo's eyes locked on to mine, and I realized that he was standing a lot closer to me than before.

His eyes lingered on mine, and I even caught them darting down to my lips. It lasted only a millisecond before he pulled his eyes back to mine but it was enough to make my heart go crazy.

I nodded and he pulled his finger back.

Something shifted in his eyes and he ripped himself from the mesmerizing daze we were both in.

He turned around and I felt like I could finally breathe. Had I even been breathing that entire time?

Focus Eden. I was getting tired of having to reprimand myself for getting distracted. I needed to get my shit together, and fast.

Apollo moved on, and I trailed close behind. The further we walked the brighter the light around us got as we made our way to the outskirts of the forest. Up ahead a light shone through the darkness.

We spilled out of the forest and found ourselves on the cusp of a huge field at the base of the Mountain of Aura.

It was the tallest thing I'd ever laid eyes on. So tall, in fact, that I had to tilt my head as far back as I could to even attempt to get a glimpse of the peak, which was impossible as it cut into the thick clouds up above.

My eyes watched as they floated carelessly on the high breeze.

Air mages really used to ride those? That far up?

I felt queasy just thinking about it. I could never.

We were to the mountain, which meant we were one step closer to finishing the mission and I was closer to a hot shower, so I was feeling ambitious and decided to head out into the field ahead of Apollo.

Who knew, maybe he would even notice my ambition and think it was admirable.

It was about time I gave him some reasons not to hate me.

I started off into the field before Apollo realized what I was doing and cried out over the open field.

"Eden stop!"

I glanced over my shoulder and furrowed my brows. For someone who was so determined and refused to put up with any nonsense he sure was taking a long time to get his shit together and make it across the field. I had simply taken it upon myself to get it going.

I was taking a jab at being bold and fearless, like Jade would. If she were there she wouldn't have hesitated. She probably would have been so bored at that point that she would have done anything to get it over with.

I was trying to bring the same energy to the table.

I took another step and a mortified look crossed Apollo's face.

There was a deafening sound, like pressurized air finally bursting out of a can, and a wave of energy blasted me into the air and sent me crashing to the ground flat of my stomach.

In an instant all the air was knocked from my lungs. It was like time slowed, and my lungs didn't even know how to work anymore thanks to the shock of the landing.

I couldn't hear a thing but the high pitched ringing in my ears. I barely had enough strength to lift my head from the ground but I managed to get it off the ground just enough for my eyes to land on what had caused the blast.

If my lungs weren't already begging for air, the sight would have taken my breath away.

In the middle of the clearing stood a huge dragon, made completely of clouds. It wasn't a fluffy, friendly looking kind either. It's head alone was the size of a few large men stacked on top of each other, and it's scales were all white. The only reason I knew it was made from clouds was the way that the pattern of it's skin shimmered beneath the scales. It reminded me of the clouds floating by slowly in the breeze.

Oh Eden, what have you gotten us into now?

Chapter 14

The dragon opened its mouth and I felt the ground vibrate beneath me.

That must have been some roar. I thought, my ears still filled with only the high pitched ring.

I flopped on my back and clawed at my chest, begging my lungs to take in a breath. Behind my eyes flashbacks of dark cold water filled my mind. I knew how it felt to suffocate, I'd done it time after time at the academy alone in the cold pool.

Work!

I beat my fist against my chest and my lungs finally caved, sucking in a sweet cool breath of air.

They were working. They burned, but that was a small price to pay.

I groaned and pushed myself to stand. Every muscle in my body was screaming and I was surprised that I hadn't broken anything. I had no idea how high the blast had rocketed me, but the ache in my chest was enough for me to decipher that it wasn't a little hop.

My eyes caught on to Apollo charging out from the woods headed straight for the dragon. He had pulled all of the water from his pouch and morphed it into a huge sword and shield, which still looked like playthings compared to the height of the dragon.

My ears slowly lost the ring, and the sound found a way to slither back to my eardrums just in time for another deafening roar to erupt from the dragon's mouth as he sliced through it's leg with his sword.

I cupped my hands over my ears.

I was right, it definitely was a roar.

The dragon's leg puffed out into a series of clouds that started to escape out onto the sky before being magically sucked back in forming the leg once again, completely undamaged.

It opened its mouth and a stream of clouds shot out that were in the shape of a stream of fire, and Apollo ducked behind his shield. The stream was so powerful that it pushed him back a few feet, even with his feet anchored solidly into the ground, leaving a train of two small grooves behind.

It was strong. Especially for something made up of clouds.

Behind it, on the rock wall of the mountain a glimmer caught my eyes. It was a mystical and shimmering yellow.

I knew in an instant that was where I needed to be. My eyes darted to Apollo and the dragon, both of which were occupied at the moment.

If there was one superpower that I was sure I had it was the power of invisibility. The only special thing about me, the power to slip in and out of places because nobody even remembered me anyway.

I hoped that it wouldn't let me down now.

I waited until they both charged at one another and I broke out into a run straight for the glow. Every bone in my body felt like it was bruised, and every muscle wanted to strangle me. I didn't even like running when I wasn't running for my life, so I was sure my body was confused.

I ran as fast as I could and managed to slip past the dragon while he was taking a swipe at Apollo with his large fangs. I made my way to the base of the mountain and saw what it was that was calling to me- a door like the ones in the temple of Eden. It held the same symbol of a cloud like the key and the box.

I instinctively reached out to touch it when my feet were swept out from underneath me and I was once again sent spiraling to the ground with the wind knocked out of me.

I looked up to see the dragon headed straight for me, my eyes wide.

I froze, it was like my body refused to cooperate when Apollo's voice found its way to me.

"Use this!" He yelled. His water pack landed right next to me. He still charged for me but the backpack made it first.

I held my hands out in front of me, with the dragon charging headfirst.

I was trying to command the water, I really was.

I strained, imagining the water coming out of the pack in my mind.

"Come on, come on!" I yelled out loud.

If there was any right time to unlock my mystical powers, it was then.

I remembered all the people who looked down on me because I couldn't command an element, and allowed myself to feel the hurt and the rage that stemmed from it. I hoped the intense emotions would open a door inside of me or something. All I knew was that I had a few seconds to learn what took people years to master otherwise I was as good as all the other edens- dead.

Beside me I could hear the water in the pack bubble and gurgle, but was it working?

I only had a few seconds left between the dragon and me.

"Come on!" I yelled so loudly that my throat stung, but it was no use.

I curled up into a ball and squeezed my eyes tightly, only left to pray for mercy, when I felt the weight of Apollo's body press up against mine.

I forced my eyes open to see Apollo on top of me, using his body to shield mine. Around us he had formed a small dome of water, hardened to protect us.

I looked up at him and he looked down at me. I was sure he'd be pissed at my cowardice, or upset that my abilities hadn't appeared when we needed them, but there wasn't a hint of anger woven into his deep blue eyes, which was a rare occurrence for him. Instead he looked down at me and I swore I saw a hint of admiration in his eyes.

Behind him I could see the dragon through the barrier, nibbling at it. Around us it vibrated and shook. But inside it felt like time slowed. I let my muscles relax into a lying position and Apollo adjusted himself, still caught on the mystical daze that hit us every time we were near one another.

"I'm sorry I couldn't do it. I really tried and it just-" My words were cut off by the warm feeling of his lips pressing firmly against mine.

It was like all my senses exploded at once, in a hyper aware burst of pleasure. My eyes widened and his closed as he melted into the kiss.

Was it actually happening? Or had I hit my head in the fall?

With my luck I was probably laying in the open field making out with nothing as Apollo watched on in horror.

Apollo pulled away with a smirk on his face.

"That's for trying." He said smoothly.

My eyes were still wide, and if I looked like a I felt there was probably a look of pure terror spread across my face.

Probably not the reaction the average guy would want at a first kiss, but it didn't phase Apollo for a second.

The dragon pulled away from the dome, probably to regroup and try a different approach, and while it did Apollo used it as a chance to pounce.

"Your only job is to open that tomb and wake Atlas up. I'll handle this guy." He sounded so determined and confident, two things that I hadn't known I was ferociously attracted to.

I simply nodded, still trying to sort out what the hell was going on and if I'd imagined the previous minute or not.

Apollo stood and the dome of water lost its shape as he commanded it back into his signature sword and shield. The dragon caught a glimpse that we were exposed and took advantage, charging us.

"Go!" Apollo yelled.

Free from the bubble of protection I saw he was back to his cold self.

It was nice while it lasted. I turned and sprinted to the door.

Like the doors in the temple of Eden it was a thick slab of rock, and it held a shimmering golden cloud that only I could see, which led me to believe that I was the only one who could open it. Even if I wanted to play the hero with brute strength like Apollo, I couldn't. That wasn't part of my story, and I had to accept it.

Behind me I heard the thundering footsteps of the dragon behind me, charging in my direction. It was clear that he was the guardian of the temple, and eden or not he didn't want me to see what was behind the door, which could only mean we were in the right place. All I had to do was figure out how to open the damn thing.

I reached out in front of me and traced my finger over the cloud out of instinct, and watched as the shimmering light disappeared.

I waited on pins and needles for the familiar sound of rock

grinding against rock like it had in the temple.

Nothing.

I glanced over my shoulder to see Apollo trying to fight the dragon off, but it was gaining ground quickly, inching closer and closer to me.

Come on, Come on. I urged the door in my mind.

The dragon was so close now that I could feel the gust of it's breath as it let out a roar.

I laid my hand over the door and yelled "Open!"

All my frustrations and emotions flowed down my arm and exploded out of my hand in a gust of wind so strong that it blasted the door backward and it hung open.

"What. The. Fuck." I muttered, looking down at my hand in awe.

Was that really me?

No tricks, no strings attached to the door, no Apollo swooping in to save me at the last minute.

All me?

I pulled myself from my thoughts and rushed inside the dark corridor just in time to hear the dragon crash into the mountain. I turned to see it yapping at the door trying to stuff itself inside, but it was too large to fit.

It pulled away, turning around probably to commence trying to destroy Apollo.

I knew I was running out of time. Apollo was strong, but he couldn't fight forever. I had to find Atlas, and I had to figure out how to wake him up.

I turned back into the dark corridor, mystical golden lights hung on either side of the hallway and glowed brighter when I passed by. It was dusty, and I had to duck more than a few times to avoid getting a face full of cobwebs.

I hurried down the hall and found that at the end it opened up to a large stone room. In the center stood a single coffin, made out of clouds that looked so soft and fluffy I almost wanted to crawl in between them and sleep for a few hundred years.

I inched closer to the coffin, wary of any more traps. I reached out, expecting my hand to go through them but was surprised to find that they were solid, almost like pillow stuffing. I pushed as hard as I could, nudging the cover all the way off and my eyes widened.

Inside lay a man resting peacefully. My eyes skimmed his features, dark brown skin, chiseled jaw, lips so lush and soft that I couldn't help imagining mine against them. I didn't think that there was another person on earth I would find as attractive as I found Apollo, but there he lay in a coffin in front of me. A perfect specimen of a man.

I reached out to touch him but before I could a small jolt of electricity jumped from my fingertips to him and his eye opened.

The first thing he saw when he awoke was me, and something inside of me stirred at the sight of his light grey eyes. There was a tingling behind my eyes. A familiar twinge of magic.

Another spark.

"My spark." He sat straight up. "You're my spark." He didn't sound upset like Apollo had, or in denial like Asher. He actually sounded happy.

Before I knew what was happening he pulled me in and laid a kiss on my lips that sent a gush of magic through my body like a title wave. I melted into this one, completely aware that he was a total stranger, but I didn't care. It felt right.

He pulled back and smiled, revealing two rows of perfect white teeth and a deep dimple in each brown cheek to match.

It was an infectious smile. I couldn't help but smile too.

Until the entire temple began to shake.

"Oh my god the dragon." I said coming back to the pain that was reality. "It's going to devour Apollo soon if we don't hurry."

"Apollo's here?" Atlas's eyes lit up at the thought of his old friend.

"Not for long if you don't call off your dragon pet out there." I stood and offered Atlas a hand.

His legs were understandably weak from a century of sleep, so I threw his arm around my shoulder and helped him inch down the corridor to the base of the cave.

In the field ahead of us the Dragon had Apollo on his back in the field, ready to rip him to shreds.

I looked up at Atlas, and watched as he pulled his fingers to his lips and a whistle pierced through the air, stopping the dragon instantly. It cocked its head to the side and rushed to him quickly.

I flinched, my first instinct to run in the opposite direction but Atlas wasn't phased.

Just as the dragon reached us it evaporated into a cloud of fog. Atlas drew in a deep breath, mystically inhaling every last inch of it.

A stillness settled over the field and I heard Apollo groan before dropping his head and panting for air in the middle of it.

"Apollo!" Atlas yelled with a chuckle. "Playing with my dragon again I see. Just like old times."

Chapter 15

I turned the faucet on and watched the water flow out in spurts, filling up the vintage bathtub in the manor.

Waves of steam rose up from it, and I sat perched on the edge in nothing but a bathrobe, mesmerized by the water.

I was exhausted, and every muscle in my body made it a point to remind me of it every chance they got. Who would have known hiking a forbidden forest and fighting a dragon made of clouds would be so draining?

There was a knock on the door and I looked up in time to see one of the maids bring in a stack of towels and dump some bubble bath into the water.

"Thank you." I said with a warm smile and she nodded.

I found myself wondering what kind of life she'd lived before she was turned to water. If she had a family, or ambitions. Surely her entire dream couldn't have been to be a maid at the manor. The place was great but it wasn't *that* great.

The bubble bath foamed, creating a thick blanket of bubbles that now floated atop the water and I decided to take the plunge.

At my home I always opted for showers, not baths. Because they were easy to work through. Showers felt like rain beating down on me, baths felt like I was soaking in a pool- and my trauma didn't play well with pools of water.

I untied my robe and let it crumple in a pile on the floor before dipping a toe into the hot water to test. When I did bathe I liked my water scalding hot. I found that the tingling of my skin was a great distraction, and worked good for keeping the bad memories at bay.

I slid into the tub sucking in air as I lowered myself into the pool of molten comfort. I let out a sigh when my body was finally submerged, only my head spared from the heat.

I couldn't believe how nice it actually felt to lay beneath the thick blanket of bubbles. I actually felt comfortable enough to close my eyes and pretend for a second that my life wasn't a complete magical mess.

I dipped a washcloth in the water, laid it over my eyes, and let out a deep sigh as I melted into the water.

"Are you enjoying yourself?" Apollo's voice came from the doorway and I flinched.

So much for relaxing.

I sat straight up, my heart pounding in my chest, and pulled the cloth from my eyes.

Apollo stood in the doorway leaned against the frame. He raised a brow at me and his cheeks burned red.

I cocked my head to the side, suddenly realizing that when I sat up I left the privacy of the thick bubbles and my breasts were completely exposed.

Apollo eyes them curiously before I leaned back into the water, frantically pulling the bubbles over me.

"I was." I groaned. "Thanks for asking."

I couldn't calm my heart that fluttered in my chest.

"Do you mind?" Apollo pointed to the chair that sat beside the tub and my cheeks blazed.

"Why not, you've already seen all there is to see of me."

"Well, not *all.*" Apollo smirked.

He took a seat in the chair and scooted it to face away from the tub in a subpar attempt to be a gentleman before he realized that all it did was tilt him toward the large mirror on the opposite side of the bathroom that was pointed directly at me.

"I tried." He muttered.

The look on his face was priceless, I never would have pegged him for the awkward type. That mixed with the hilarity of the situation was too much for me, and I caught myself laughing. It was only a chuckle at first, but it found a way to morph into an all out, tears streaming down my face, laugh.

It was contagious too. No matter how hard Apollo tried to steady his normally icy glare his lips curled at the edges before he erupted in a fit of laughter too.

It felt good to laugh, and not the awkwardly obligated kind. An actual, real laugh.

"We almost got killed today." I managed to say in between chuckles.

"The world could have ended." Apollo said mid laugh.

"And we *kissed!*" The word only made me laugh harder, until I realized that Apollo had stopped.

A thick layer of awkwardness filled the room as I tried to calm my laughter.

I looked into the mirror and my eyes met Apollo's before he quickly darted them away.

"I don't know what came over me when that happened." Each word was like a knife in my stomach. "I couldn't control myself, but it was a mistake."

The words stung my skin even more than the singe of the water did.

"Right." I rushed to the word too quickly. "Yeah, totally."

I turned away, suddenly deeply interested in soaking my washcloth and running it over my arms and neck, all while blinking back tears.

"That's what I was about to say." I lied.

My stomach sunk and my confidence was in shreds. Just when I was starting to settle into the thought of my new life, and my new purpose.

Just when I was about to get some freaking relaxation.

The tension in the room was anything but relaxing, it was unnerving in fact.

"Was that what you came in here to tell me?" I snapped.

"I came in to see if you were doing okay." Apollo said, his tone slipping into defensive territory.

"Well I'm fine. Obviously. So you can go."

"Eden don't be like that." Apollo sighed and rubbed his hand over his face in frustration.

"Go!" I yelled and a rush of energy swept through me and came out as a gust of wind that was so powerful it knocked Apollo off of his chair and sent him spiraling to the ground.

My mouth hung open, in awe at what I'd done, but Apollo didn't share my enthusiasm. He jumped up and huffed angrily as he made his way out the door, slamming it behind him.

I sat in the warm water, trying to wrap my head around the roller coaster of events that had transpired.

Was that gust of wind actually me?

That mixed with what happened earlier at the Mountain of Aura was enough to sway my opinion.

Maybe I still had a chance at becoming the magical eden everyone thought I could be.

***

I found Atlas meditating in the backyard. He levitated a few feet off the ground, cross legged beside the temple. The warm tone of the sunset only complimented his dark complexion. His skin glowed and his features were soft. He looked as peaceful and relaxed as I'd wished I was.

He heard me approaching and descended back into a seated position on the ground. Even the grey tones of his eyes sparkled in the fading sunlight.

A wide smile spread across his face revealing his dimples. Something inside me swooned at the sight. He was actually excited to see me, which was more than I could say for Apollo- and I'd known him longer.

"Well hello." He said, lips still pulled tightly in a smile. "I was hoping you'd come and find me."

"Oh yeah?" I smiled nervously and brushed a lock of brown hair behind my ear.

Atlas was the polar opposite of Apollo, I could already tell. He was warm and soft by default- loving and happy.

I doubted that Apollo even knew the meaning of some of those words.

Atlas patted his hand against the lush grass beside him, inviting me to sit, which I happily obliged. It felt good to actually feel like my presence was welcomed. My entire life felt like the feeling you get when you walk into a room and someone immediately gets up and walks out. Rejected, unwanted, and unloved.

Even Apollo's interactions with me felt obligated. He needed me to help him save the world, maybe that was all I was to him - a tool. A weapon he could use to vanquish his enemies then discard back into the weapons room without a second thought.

Atlas felt different. Even the pull I felt to him felt warmer and more genuine. I knew he would never try to downplay the kiss we shared.

"What were you doing?" I asked, mostly out of genuine curiosity but partly to take off some of the pressure of how deeply he was staring into my soul.

"I was listening to the air." He said melodically.

My brow furrowed as I tried to understand how someone could listen to the air.

I opened my mouth to ask but Atlas shushed me with a smile and held out his hand. "You're an eden, so you have the power to hear it too."

I thought for a moment, hesitant to grab his hand. Not because of the contact, but because I had gotten my hopes up so many times before. I'd gotten to the place where I finally believed that I could be the savior that everyone needed, only for them to be shattered.

Did I dare believe in myself?

That was a question that had plagued me for my entire life. It followed me everywhere I went and nagged me for everything I did. Whether it was school, work at the brew, or even just deeming myself worthy to be friends with Jade.

Did I dare let myself feel a glimmer of hope? Was it too crazy to throw in a splash of confidence?

I thought back to a few minutes ago when Apollo had shattered my being with a few small words, and I felt a familiar sense of anger in the pit of my stomach.

Why did I do that? What inside me was so broken that I let

myself rely on other people for every ounce of confidence that I had?

All that led to was a string of tears and broken hearts.

I slipped my hand into Atlas's and he wove his fingers in between mine.

I looked up at him with a fire in my eyes. I was done letting other people define me. It was time for Eden Montgomery to define herself.

Atlas smiled knowingly, like he felt not only felt the shift inside of me, but approved of it.

He closed his eyes and I did the same.

"When you take away one sense, the rest are heightened. For mages, this is even more so." Atlas's voice made its way to my ears in smooth waves. "Just calm your mind, and allow yourself to feel what needs to be seen."

His wording confused me, but I was determined to make it work, so I took a deep breath and let my mind fall still.

Around me I heard the rustling of leaves in the breeze, and a few birds chirped from the forest that surrounded us. It was peaceful and it was calm, but most importantly it was relaxing. I was actually the most relaxed that I'd been, probably in my entire life.

I noticed more subtle nuances throughout my body, places in my back and my neck that my muscles were clinging to tension that I hadn't realized before. Most of all, though, my sense of touch was heightened. I could feel every dip in Atlas's hand that clung to mine. I was hyper aware of the way it felt for our skin to brush together, and how tightly he squeezed my hand.

"Don't be distracted by your senses, lean into them." Atlas's words only lasered my focus. "The elements are living magical beings, contrary to popular belief."

His words struck me. I'd never heard it phrased like that before. I'd always viewed them as concrete things, not alive, not dead, just *there*.

"It is said that they choose who to share their power with. The wind has the power to carry sounds and voices. Its gusts travel the globe, and as air mages we have the privilege to share in its power too. You just have to accept it."

Voices? My thoughts raced. *Does that mean I could hear Jade?*

My attention fluttered and Atlas squeezed my hand, pulling me back to our concentration.

I took a deep breath and leaned into my other senses.

"Air, I accept my power." I said quietly, my voice almost a whisper. "I want to hear Jade."

A sudden rush of wind blew over us filled with an array of voices, all speaking at once. I couldn't make out a single word until they all dropped and only one remained. The sound of a woman crying.

Jade.

I opened my eyes and realized that we were floating, just as I was spiraling to the earth.

I landed roughly on my butt, but jumped up quickly.

Atlas floated down gently and opened his eyes.

"What is it?" He asked.

"We need to wake up the last carrier. NOW. Jade needs me."

Chapter 16

Apollo, Atlas, and I all filed into the small stone temple. I had thought it was a tight fit before, but now with three people it seemed even smaller.

Atlas stood close behind me, his body pushing up against mine. I squirmed at the touch and Apollo noticed, raising a brow.

That wasn't a glint of jealousy in his eyes, was it?

I pushed the thought from my mind. It was impossible. He'd made it crystal clear how he felt about me- about us- a mistake.

"Why the sudden push to awaken the last carrier?" Apollo asked, brow still raised. There was a hint of disdain in his voice.

"Because, I heard Jade." I said, ignoring the look of surprise on his face. "She's out there, she's alive, and she needs me. It seems like the only way that's going to happen and I'm going to have any chance against Asher is by waking the last carrier up. I need to crack the code to my powers."

"Looks to me like you've had no problem unlocking your air magic." Apollo huffed and crossed his arms, trying his best to make his anger look casual.

It was anything but.

I rolled my eyes. I didn't have time for drama, and I definitely didn't have time to stress over someone who had made it completely obvious how they felt about me.

"Let's just work on the next carrier."

I moved to the last solid stone door in the temple, staring intently.

I expected to see something- anything that would give me a clue on how to open it. Instead I was met with the grey stone door. No mystical lights, no magical bread crumbs, nothing.

I sighed.

Of course the last door would give me a hard time, because the universe was snarky and never could cut me a break.

Just when I was about to turn around and declare defeat there was a sound that came from inside. It was a small scratching noise, like tiny claws.

"Do you guys hear that?" I pressed my ear up against the cool rock and the noise grew louder.

Judging by the looks that they exchanged I guessed that I had either gone crazy, or fallen victim to yet another magical occurrence.

I pulled my ear from the rock and inspected the door once again, with no sign of magic in sight.

I groaned, the fire to find Jade still burning hot in the pit of my stomach with no outlet to escape.

"Maybe it's not time for us to wake Adler up yet." Apollo said, with a hint of insecurity in his cold voice.

I shot him a dissatisfied look and his face hardened.

"I said maybe."

Eye roll.

I thought back to what I'd learned throughout my years in the academy. As an outcast I always had to work twice as hard to prove myself whether it was magical homework, or just trying to make friends. What did I take away?

There's always another way to do something if you search hard enough.

A glint of light caught my eye. It shone from beneath the door, inching its way through a small crack. It called to me like light called to a moth, beckoning me to find it.

The guys looked at me like I was crazy when I dropped to my stomach and pressed my eye up against the crack but I didn't care. I didn't have time for the universe's riddles.

I was nearly blinded by the light that flooded through, but I also felt a small gust of wind trickle through with it.

I jumped to my feet and searched the rest of the door before I sprinted outside.

If a draft was wafting from the inside, there had to be a way for it to get in.

The guys followed- Apollo reluctantly and Atlas curiously.

I rounded the large building until I got to the corner that lined up with the temple and a smile spread across my face. Three beams of light lined up perfectly like the outline of a door in an otherwise seamless wall.

"Got you." I smirked.

One upping the universe was beginning to be my thing.

In the center of the outline was the familiar symbol of a leaf and I traced it with my fingertip. The rocks vibrated and the wall caved in revealing a solid rock door that was hidden within.

I turned to Apollo and smiled smugly.

I was finding out that when you let yourself speak your mind once, it was hard to quiet the voice again. It got louder and louder every time I indulged myself- let my outsides match my insides.

Somewhere deep inside I knew my days of being a pushover were coming to a close, and I wasn't sad about it at all.

I pranced inside the temple. The walls were covered with strings of magical glowing green ivy. They crawled up the wall and tangled over one another on the ceiling. In the center of it all was the earth shrine. My eyes fell on the mystical green treasure chest, it called to me just as much as the others had. Only this time it didn't have a keyhole.

I inched closer and realized that there was an inscription etched into the lid in shimmering letters.

What is greater than the gods, and more evil than the devil?
The poor have it, and the rich need it.

If you eat it, you will die.

I mouthed the words as I ran my fingertip over top of them.

Apollo and Atlas inched closer too, until they were each so close that I could feel their warm breath on either side of my neck.

Both of them so close to me made my stomach twitch and sent a shiver up my spine. Both of them, together, awakened a longing for each of them more powerful than any I'd felt. It was like the magic inside of me could sense the magic inside of them, and for a split second all I could think about was all of us naked.

How good it would feel to have both sets of hands roam the crevices of my bare body at the same time.

Eden!

The thought was far too bold, even for the Eden I was becoming.

"A riddle." Apollo huffed.

"This was definitely Adler's idea." Atlas sounded impressed.

"Wait, they let him decide?" Apollo pulled away.

"Well yeah. Me too, you think they just chose a cloud dragon to protect my tomb?"

"What!" Apollo fumed. "I didn't get a say-"

"Nothing." I cut Apollo off.

The words tumbled from my lips as I worked through the riddle.

"What?" They both said in unison.

"The answer to the riddle. It's nothing."

A smile spread across Atlas' lips and he sunk his teeth into his bottom one. His eyes said it all. If he wasn't attracted to me before, he damn sure was now.

He eyed me hungrily.

I guess we know brains are attractive to him. I felt myself blush.

I glanced at Apollo and he rolled his eyes.

If only I knew what was attractive to Apollo.

The chest vibrated and shook, returning my focus to the task at hand.

The lid popped open and a blinding green light shone from inside. The mystical light was shaped into the form of a small mouse and it darted out of the box, climbed down the wall and disappeared in a small hole at the base of it.

"That explains the scratching noise." I said, my eyes falling on a small piece of paper that lay inside it.

"Proceed to level two?" I read aloud, confusion on my lips. "What does that—"

My words were spliced short by the rumble of rock beneath our feet. Before I knew what was going on the floor caved in beneath us and we fell. I felt the smooth embrace of a slide catch me and I slipped further and further into the darkness.

I felt like I was a kid at a park, except the slide we shot down twisted and turned deep into the earth, and all I could see was pitch black.

A scream erupted from my lips as we fell sliding into darkness, before the trail spit us out at the bottom.

I skitted across a jagged stone floor, my eyes rushing to adjust to the soft light of the torches that clung to the walls of the long stone hallway we were in.

A smile clung to my face at the rush. I hated to admit it but the ride down was kind of fun. I hadn't felt that tickling feeling in the pit of my stomach in a long time.

"That lazy bastard had them encase him underneath the temple?" Apollo got to his feet and brushed the dust from his clothes.

"Oh boo." I teased and Apollos cheeks blazed red. "I thought it was fun. Don't be a party pooper."

"Yeah Apollo, don't be a party pooper." Atlas echoed.

My comments only mentally solidified my theory that once you let yourself not give a shit it was hard not to do it over and over.

I wasn't complaining, I kind of liked it. Saying what I felt, but even when the bravery to do that became easier and easier I still felt the nag of anxiety in the back of my mind. I was sure that I would rethink all of my words as I laid in bed that night, but in the moment I didn't care about that either.

"Let's go find this guy."

I made my way down the hallway, marveling at the mystical torches that clung to the walls and lit the way. Their warm golden ambiance filled the stone hallway. I was actually glad that he'd thought of them, because neither of us had flashlights with us and we would have been royally screwed. The hallway was long and only wide enough for us to work our way through single file.

When I got to the end I paused, glancing down both sides of the intersection that it branched off into.

Right? Or left?

I decided to go left, which after a few twists and turns I realized was the wrong choice.

A dead end. I groaned.

"You really know what you're doing here, huh?" Apollo criticized.

I didn't think it was possible for him to get even more hostile and sarcastic but he proved me wrong when Atlas joined our unofficial crew. I didn't even want to imagine what he'd be like when we woke Adler.

God forbid anyone show me any type of attention.

We all spun around, which put Apollo in the front.

"There you go. You show us which way to go big guy." Atlas pat him on the back, which obviously rubbed Apollo the wrong way.

"I will." He grumbled and led us. We got to the cross in the road and he turned down the hallway we'd originally come from.

After a few steps when he noticed neither Atlas or I was following him he realized his mistake.

"Nice work genius." Atlas smiled.

I giggled quietly behind him. I didn't want to admit it to myself, but in a way it was funny to see him so mad. I liked the way Atlas teased him. They reminded me of two brothers squabbling.

Atlas took the lead and Apollo and I followed.

I felt like Atlas was in his area of expertise. Every time we got to a crossroads in the maze he stopped, took a breath, and listened. I knew he was using his magic to get an edge over the riddle of the maze, but it was only fair.

Every turn he took that didn't lean to a dead end made Apollo fume even more. I could basically feel it radiating off of him as he trailed closely behind me.

He'd get over it.

Something told me that these guys were trying to outdo each other long before I was ever in the picture. Plus, a little rivalry was healthy.

Right?

Chapter 17

"So, Apollo," Atlas called from ahead of me to Apollo who walked closely behind me. "Eden, she woke you first?" His voice was thick with curiosity.

"Actually-" I was about to correct him when Apollo cut me off.

"Yeah. Just before she woke you." Apollo tied.

I glanced over my shoulder at him and raised a brow.

Why not just tell the truth?

Apollo made it a point to avert his eyes from mine, pretending that the ivy that climbed the rocks had piqued his interest so I turned my attention back to the front.

We had a mission at hand, plus I had a perfect view of Atlas's gloriously toned ass, so I wasn't about to complain.

"What's it like?" Atlas continued as we rounded another corner. "The world I mean. Is it as chaotic as when we left it?"

Apollo huffed. "It's worse. Far worse."

I thought about his words and the only world I'd ever known. A world of peace and harmony didn't even feel real to me. I didn't know if something like that had even ever existed, despite his tales of the past. Even more so I doubted if it did if I'd ever witness it's return in my future.

My life was just one string of chaotic events after another, even before either of them. Far before I knew I had any magical powers at all I sat at the eye of a tornado of chaos and called it home. I didn't know anything else, and I wasn't sure if I even wanted to.

We turned a corner and Atlas stopped abruptly, sending me bumping into him. He glanced over his shoulder and smirked at me. Something told me that my body pressed tightly against his wasn't something that he was going to complain about.

My cheeks burned red as I blushed and backed up a little to give him some room, only to back right into Apollo.

My ass pressed firmly against his crotch and even underneath his pants I could feel the bulge of his cock pressing flaccidly against the fabric.

My cheeks burned even brighter.

"I'm sorry." I mumbled, flustered.

"Don't be." They both said in unison and turned their attention back to what lay ahead of us, something I was still struggling with.

I peaked over Atlas's shoulder to see that the floor of the hallway ahead of us had turned into a murky pool of water that spanned for about twenty feet ahead of us. Beneath the water something stirred.

Just when I was about to ask what it was I leaped up and took a snap at us.

Atlas jumped back, pushing me into Apollo. This time all three of our bodies pressed together, with me sandwiched in between the two of them. It was definitely the sexiest sandwich I'd ever had the pleasure of making, but there were more important issues at hand.

When the creature left up from the water it revealed its mystical green body and I realized what it was- a crocodile made of vines.

It's eyes glowed a shade of green that matched the color of the magic that had escaped the chest when I broke the riddle.

It was so bright it captivated my attention. My eyes looked onto it and I felt like I couldn't look away no matter how hard I tried.

"What is that thing?"

"Another one of Adler's tests. He loves tests and riddles, as I'm sure you can guess by now." Apollo's lips were so close to my ear that I could feel the wisps of his breath brush against it.

I was ashamed to say that the feeling was turning me on, awakening an ache inside of me that I'd never felt before all of this started.

Sex was the furthest thing from my mind before my life started to fall apart. A boyfriend? Maybe. But the actual sex part of a relationship just wasn't something that had called to me- but then I met the guys and it was like something that as dormant in my body had awoken.

And it was all I could think about every time we touched.

I wanted it so bad. Almost as badly as I needed to eat or breathe, and that was a new and terrifying feeling for me.

Apollo reached out his hand in the direction of the water and used his magic to solidify it into a block of solid ice, trapping the water beneath the thick sheet of it.

Atlas took the first step, then another and another and I followed closely behind. Beneath us the gator banged on the sheet of ice, each thump sending a crack spidering out across it.

We moved as quickly as we could over it and I breathed a sigh of relief. I didn't know how long the sheet of ice would last, but. I was sure that we wanted to be far from it by the time it finally caved and broke. Fighting a mystical crocodile wasn't necessarily on the list of things that I wanted to do that day.

We took a few winds and turns and I finally let myself breathe out a sigh of relief. Just as I did Atlas once again planted his feet firmly on the ground and I bumped into him, which made Apollo bump into me.

Another sexy Eden sandwich.

"What is it this time?" I asked, trying to distract myself from the growing wetness between my legs.

"Another Adler booby trap."

Up ahead the floor of the hallway had gone missing and in its place was an indent in the floor filled with sharpened spears that stuck straight up.

I gulped.

I was glad that Atlas was leading. Knowing me I would have clumsily stumbled into both of the traps, most likely leading us to our own deaths.

I still had a lot to learn.

Atlas reached out and from his hand summoned a bridge of solid cloud, and as we walked over it I realized that statement also applied to my magical abilities. If I truly had the power to control each element then I was a long way from mastering each, and that was if I was being generous with myself. It took some people a lifetime to master one- I had to master four before the unknown demise of civilization that was slowly creeping up on us.

No pressure.

Finally we took a turn and the hallway opened up into a large enclosed area. It was as big as the room that I'd stumbled upon Atlas in.

Just like the temple above us and the hallways strings of Ivy crawled up the walls and wove together to cover the ceiling.

It looked like something you'd find deep in the jungle, not burrowed underneath the ground.

The ivy glowed the same shade of mystical green as before, it was actually quite breathtaking. It shed it cast its light over everything in the room leaving it with a green tint.

In the center of the room stood a coffin completely encased in ivy.

"This is it? It seems a little too easy, doesn't it?" As soon as the words fell from my lips the room began to shake and Apollo shot an angry glare my way.

"Thanks Eden."

I smiled nervously.

Of course. Just doing what I always do.

The stone around us vibrated and rumbled so loudly that I was afraid that an earthquake was coming, which obviously isn't something you want to happen when you're fifty feet underneath the surface of the earth.

Before your eyes we watched as the ivy fed from the ceiling in strands, but instead of hitting the floor it began to clump together in the center of the room.

Please don't be a dragon. Please don't be a dragon. Please don't be a dragon. I pleaded with the universe.

I watched in both awe and horror as the vines clumped and twisted to take on a humanoid shape. It was about as tall as two men, and it was thick.

I stared at the giant, and just when I was about to try to convince myself that it wasn't very bad it opened its mouth and let out a thundering roar.

It's definitely bad.

On one side of me I saw Apollo pull water from his pouch and form his familiar sword. On the other I noticed Atlas with his hands out at either side of his and felt a small breeze against my skin. I looked over to see him hovering amidst a small tornado that engulfed his feet. He took in it, and used it to gently glide back and forth. It kind of reminded me of a skateboard or a scooter, just a magical one. I looked up to see that his eyes had gone all white- pupil, iris, and all.

It was a scarily attractive sight.

One look and I knew he was someone I never wanted to cross in battle.

Apollo and Atlas looked at each other like old friends and I got the feeling that this wasn't their first rodeo running into battle together. Their gaze turned to me and we all nodded, finally *all* on the same wavelength.

They fight, I wake up Adler.

That was the plan.

I watched as they charged forward and the monster charged at them too. Apollo immediately swung his sword and connected with the monster's forearm slicing it off cleanly. It thudded to the ground solidly before smile vines emerged from it's wound and formed another one.

Crap.

Atlas charged the monster and created a small tornado that spun it in circles. I was watching closely when I realized something was moving out of the corner of my eye- the arm.

More vines had emerged from the clean edge of the cut and it had grown into another vine monster- and it was looking directly at me.

Of course.

My eyes darted from the monster at the edge of the room, to the coffin that sat dead center, and back. It saw me and it followed my gaze to the coffin.

These were more than just beasts, they were intelligent creatures.

Even though I'd never met Adler I felt like going through his maze and meeting the beasts he'd created to guard him had told me more about him than anyone else could.

He was clever.

And I was impressed.

That was a turn on that I didn't know I had until I ran into it face first.

There I stood with no weapon, no plan, and magical powers so minuscule that they wouldn't be of any use to me any time soon.

But that wasn't the point of the maze. It wasn't brute strength- it was a test of wits, and thankfully that was something that I had.

I turned and ran back down the hallway in the opposite direction.

I breathed a sigh of relief that Atlas's cloud bridge still stood solidly over the spear trap. I sprinted over it and made my way to the murky ice covered water. I used the heel of my shoe to smash the ice, spreading the crack that crept across its surface until it snapped.

The crocodile wasted no time smashing through to the surface and nipping at me.

"Here crocodile." I taunted. "I'm going to pillage your temple."

The croc snapped at me, and I jumped backward. It dragged itself from the depths of the water and waddled surprisingly fast after me as I ran back into the enclosure. It nipped at my heels, close on my tail. I charged toward the monster and slid between its legs, leading the crocodile right to it. It tried to bite me, but instead clamped down on the beasts ankle.

A thundering roar emerged from it's mouth and I watched as the beast swung at the crocodile.

That should entertain them both.

I looked up to see Apollo glance at me with an impressed smirk on his face and my skin tingled at the sight.

I reclaimed my attention. I didn't know how long I had, so I bolted to the coffin and ripped the vines from it before pushing away the heavy stone slab that laid on top of it.

Inside lay Adler. He was shirtless, and I couldn't help but admire the muscles that rippled underneath the skin of his toned chest. His skin was fair, and he had jet black hair. Tattoos of ivy crawled up both of his arms like the ivy crawled up the walls of the temple.

He was captivating, just as Atlas had been.

The second the coffin opened the bright green magic seeped out of the beasts and flowed into Adler bringing him to life.

He opened his hooded eyes, which had a distinct curve, revealing two deep pools of brown.

The second they landed on me he smiled and I felt the familiar buzz of magic behind mine.

Another spark.

"You're one clever chick."

I glanced around and nervously smiled.

Before I could utter a single thank you the walls around us started to shake.

"We have to go." I offered a hand and pulled him from his place.

Atlas and Apollo had already made their way to the opposite side of the large room. I watched as Apollo used his water sword to hack away at the ivy to reveal another path- a staircase that led up, hopefully to the surface.

We darted up the staircase and my thighs burned, punishing me for all the times I'd promised them I'd work out but never did.

Around us the temple crumbled, even the walls of the staircase caved in. A small light shone at the top and it grew bigger the closer we got.

We spilled out onto the surface just in time, panting in the soft grass and bathing in the light of the full moon. We had come out at the rocky base of a cliff not far from the manor, embedded in the woods that surrounded it.

Adler looked over at me, with shadows cast across his face from the moonlight. "That was one hell of a first date if you ask me."

Apollo groaned from somewhere behind me.

Chapter 18

I tossed and turned amid the silk sheets of my bed- drifting in and out of sleep. Johnathon had given me the largest suite in the house. He had said that it was meant for an eden, and only edens had ever occupied it.

Just like I'd predicted my mind was set ablaze by the day's events. I lay awake, running over everything that had happened- silently cringing at every bold thing I'd said.

It felt good to let myself run with the truth for a while. There was a part of me that I would say even enjoyed telling people where they could shove it, but my mind always found its way back to it's anxious default. As a result I laid awake, mentally kicking myself for being *too rude* or *too straightforward.*

Old habits die hard, and this one held on for dear life.

I hated that I constantly searched for a reason, big or small, to tear myself to shreds. I was my own worst enemy, and I always had been.

I groaned and pulled myself up to sit.

There was no escaping my mind, but maybe I could occupy it for at least a few minutes.

An eerie gust of cool air brushed over my bare legs and I shivered before I pulled a bathrobe over my shoulders and cinched it tightly at the waist.

Note to self, shorts and a tank top aren't the best choice of nightwear in a drafty old manor.

The room looked increasingly different with nothing but the pale moonlight that flooded in through the window to guide me. The dark seemed to skew my recollection of where exactly the bedroom door sat, and I found myself colliding face first with a solid wall.

I rubbed at my nose sorely, glad that none of the guys were there to witness the blunder. With my hands out in front of me, I slid my fingertips lightly over the wall, feeling for the door.

If I didn't know better I would have swore I felt a low vibration coursing through the walls. But that couldn't be right. No matter how hard I racked my brain I couldn't think of a reason why the walls would be humming so much. It vibrated through my hands so heavily that they tingled.

It was the wee hours of the morning, and I was running off of god knows how many hours without sleep. Not to mention the slew of life changes that were easily enough to push someone to the edge of their sanity, so I brushed it off. At that point I was so exhausted, both physically and mentally, that I wasn't even completely sure if I was dreaming or not. I was at a point in my life where nothing would surprise me, there wasn't a trick the universe had left in it's bag that could catch me off guard.

I took a few cautious steps, careful not to let my own feet betray me and send me spiraling to the harsh floor, when my fingers caught on a small dip in the wall, It was a circular divot where it felt like someone had wallpapered over a hole in the wall that hadn't been fixed.

I had no idea why I did it, or what came over me, but I pressed my fingertip against it, ripping through the pale floral wallpaper.

I cringed at the sound, hoping that Johnathon wasn't too attached to it. My mind immediately jumped to all the ways I could pawn it off on someone else. I settled that I could say that it was like that when I first came into the room, and was just about to pull my finger from the hole when I felt something smooth and round inside- a button.

And when you find a secret button hidden in a magical manor at three in the morning and you haven't slept enough to form a logical thought in your mind there's only one thing you can do- push it.

Beside me there was a rumbling sound, followed by a small crack of light piercing through the thick darkness. I knew it wasn't the door. If my suspicions were true that was on the opposite wall, but I did remember seeing an antique bookcase against the other wall.

The small sparkle of light grew bigger and bigger, starting as a sliver and eventually growing to an all out beam. As the beam of light grew bigger the darkness that once blanketed the room grew thinner and thinner until I was able to make out my surroundings. I watched as the bookcase slowed to a stop, quietly relishing in the fact that I was right.

It continued to slide out like a door on a hinge, until it ground to a halt. I was surprised that the entire house hadn't heard it, but I had no doubts in my mind that everyone else was fast asleep. Not everyone was tortured by their own thoughts on a constant basis. Normal people actually slept during these hours.

But on the other hand I wasn't sure if it was safe to consider the three supernatural mages who happened to also be my fated mates fell under the category of *normal* people.

If this had happened even just a week earlier there wouldn't have been a chance on the entire magical earth that I would drag my booty into a mysterious corridor hidden by a fake bookshelf, but in that moment I could say that it wasn't even the most peculiar or even the most intimidating thing that I had done.

The light called to me in ways that I didn't understand, like the way the lights in the temple of eden did. It was like something was so magically intertwined in my being that it sucked me in, and I didn't have a say whether I wanted to follow it's beckon or not, my body made the decision for me.

I stepped inside the stone corridor that smelled like earth and moss, and the bookcase slowly closed behind me. The dancing white flames of the torches that lined each wall caught my eye. They bobbed and weaved mystically.

I took a few steps down the hall, cautiously watching each one. Adler's maze had ruined secret passageways for me, probably forever.

I rounded the corner and found a wooden slate among the stone wall with a button located next to it.

Let's see where you turn out.

I pressed the button and another grinding sound filled the air. I watched as the wooden slat swung out, just like the bookcase had, and it revealed the large kitchen. I slipped through the crack and realized that it wasn't just a slat, it was the backside of the grand china cabinet. I had noticed it when Johnathon had first given me a tour of the manor, mainly because it held such intricate carvings in its wood.

I spun around, a thirst for more exploration of the manor filling me when I stopped in my tracks.

Standing in front of the fridge was Adler, his arms full of food and a slice of summer sausage hanging halfway out of his mouth.

His eyes were wide, but I was sure mine were too.

The soft light from inside the refrigerator washed over half of his face and cast deep shadows over the other half, further highlighting the shape cut of his jaw bone.

Does this guy ever wear a shirt? My eyes roamed the bare skin of his chest, I couldn't help it. It was a temptation that I couldn't overcome, and I wasn't sure if I wanted to.

"I, uhhh, I'm just-" I stammered, trying to find some plausible explanation for my mysterious appearance putting a damper on his midnight snack.

"The coolest chick ever!" Adler smiled so widely that the summer sausage slipped from his lips and met an untimely end on the kitchen floor.

He nudged the refrigerator door closed with his foot and flicked on a light, careful not to let another precious ounce of food slip from his grasp.

"Solving riddles in sacred temples, mystically appearing from mysterious secret passages, you kick ass Eden Montgomery." He shoved two slices of sausage into his mouth, presumably to make up for the one he'd missed out on and plopped down at the kitchen table.

I had to admit that those were words I wasn't used to hearing all thrown into the same sentence. I most definitely wasn't used to people telling me that I was cool, or that I kicked ass.

"Do you mind if I join you?" I asked, already pulling up a chair.

The sight of all his delicious bounty made me realize how empty my own stomach was.

He nodded and pushed me a pack of crackers, which I gladly opened. I liked how laid back he was. He gave off calm vibes, unlike the chaos that vibrated off of Apollo. Apollo's chaos didn't play very well with mine.

I always ended up feeling anxious and high strung when I was around him. Adler had the opposite effect on me.

"Tell me, are you always this hungry at three in the morning?" I asked before sliding a cracker into my mouth, and relishing the salty goodness.

"Not necessarily." Adler laughed. "But I did sleep for almost a hundred years. After that long a guy is bound to have an appetite, right?"

"I would guess so." I smiled as I watched him devour the food.

I watched the pleasure that eating brought him, and realized that it was probably the most excitement that he'd seen in a long time.

"My family," Adler managed to slip the words through a full mouth. "They loved food. It was our thing. Birthdays, New Years, holidays, everything was celebrated by food. It's my happy place."

A glint of sadness glittered in his eyes.

I'd almost forgotten everyone he knew from before was dead, and with them probably everything he'd ever loved.

You wouldn't have been able to tell just based on his goofy demeanor. He seemed like a happy person, and he worked hard to hide it, but every once in a while when he slipped up you could see it in his eyes. It was there for a second, and gone as fast as it had come but I knew from experience that it was still in there, festering and growing beneath his happiness.

My heart hurt for him. I knew better than anyone the gaping hole that not having a family left inside you. I had barely even known mine. I couldn't imagine what it must have felt like to have bonded with a family only to have the cruel events of the world force them so far away from you.

"So, Miss Eden," Adler straightened his back and did an

impersonation of Johnathon that made me snort embarrassingly. "Tell me about yourself. I know you're my spark and all, but you're going to have to put in work if you want this heart girlfriend." He snapped his fingers and sunk his teeth into a peanut butter sandwich.

An awkward laugh joined the ranks of my embarrassing snort, but I didn't even care. I could tell Adler was the type of person that not only made you feel like it was okay to act like an idiot, but joined in on the idiocy with you.

It was refreshing.

"Well..." I searched my mind. The question had caught me off guard.

Up until that moment people had been telling me about my life. Whether it was my destiny, or my mysterious past. Apollo and Johnathon basically filled me in on my own life. Even Atlas had taught me about my ability to command the air, which I was slowly learning to become comfortable with.

But Adler? He was the only one who took the time to stop the clock on the ominous impending doom to ask me about myself.

And it had me dumbfounded. Every piece of information I'd ever known flew out of my brain. It was a blank slate.

Adler raised a perfectly carved brow. "Okay, let's start with an easier one. Middle name- go!"

"Rose." I said matter of factly. "I don't really know why my mother chose it, because I never really knew her. But when I was a kid I told myself that it was because that was the flower my father had brought to her because he was so happy when he'd found out she was pregnant."

"Wow, okay, you just slapped me in the face with a lot of information there." Adler blinked. "See, I knew you had it in that pretty little head of yours. You just have to be more sure of yourself is all."

His words made my cheeks tingle, and I darted my eyes away from his.

"Okay Okay. What about you?"

"Adler Jackson Fox, and I don't have the slightest clue why." He made his way back to the fridge, strategically shoving the food back into it just well enough that it would come toppling out for the next person that dared open it up. "But that's all you're getting from me without a date." He topped his words off with a wink. "Goodnight Eden Rose." He uttered before he disappeared around the corner leaving me with nothing but my thoughts.

"Goodnight Adler Jackson."

Chapter 19

I sat alone in the kitchen with my thoughts, trying to sort them out. I didn't know why but my mind always seemed to feel the clearest in the early hours of the morning. There was something about the stillness that blanketed everything around me like a fresh white coat of snow. When everyone was fast asleep I didn't have anyone's standards to try to live up to but my own.

I boiled some tea and sat with the warm glass cupped between both hands. I let its comforting heat wash over me in waves.

When I'd first arrived at the manor I was in complete denial. I couldn't see a way that any of the things that Apollo and Johnathon were saying could have possibly been about me. I couldn't even begin to imagine myself as anything other than the broken invisible girl that everyone in the town loved to hate.

But after the moment Adler and I shared I felt my feelings begin to stir. I definitely wasn't in love with him. I barely knew him, but there was no denying the magical connection we shared. The fated spark that left its imprint on us both. It was the same one I shared with Apollo and Atlas. I couldn't explain it, and I had no doubt that the girl I was a week ago would have adamantly denied it too, but I believed it now. I didn't know if it was the magic of the early morning, or the ability to be alone with the quiet of my mind but I could almost feel it- the magic- coursing through my veins.

I sipped on my tea and let the hot liquid soothe my soul from the inside out. I was a firm believer that there wasn't a problem in the world that a properly brewed cup of tea couldn't solve.

I was slowly adapting to the chaos that had become my life, and I began to feel more and more like myself with every obstacle that I overcame. Maybe there was more to me than even I was letting myself believe.

Amidst the silence I caught a glimpse of light shining brightly behind the china cabinet out of the corner of my eye. After everything that I'd been through it was obvious that it was the beckon of magic, calling to me.

And there, alone in the dark, I decided to answer it.

It was time to see what I was made of, who I was without Apollo, or Atlas, or even Adler there to bail me out.

I found the small button beside the cabinet hidden just beneath the surface of the wallpaper just like the last. one. I took a deep breath and pressed it firmly before slipping through the opening and glancing around the stone passageway. It was just as I had left it before Adler had distracted me from my exploration. But this time a bright white light glowed, its rays coming from further down the path nearly lost behind the corner. Its glow called to me even more intensely than any of the others. It unsettled something deep inside me and seemed familiar all at once.

It felt like a song that you hear. The kind that you vaguely remember but you don't know where from, that still manages to pull decades of nostalgia from inside you. One you can almost place, but can't seem to get off of the tip of your tongue.

Behind my eyes flashes of memories that I didn't know I had darted past. They were there in a second and gone the next.

I couldn't shake the overwhelming feeling that I'd not only been there before, but more than once.

The revelation didn't make any sense to me, but I followed the glow anyway. I rounded the corner and it seemed like just as I was about to steal a glimpse at it, it darted around another winding corner, just out of my sight.

It was playing a game with me, one that I didn't know the rules to. I wasn't entirely sure what it was or why it wanted me, but still I followed.

"Eden." A disembodied whisper bounced off of the walls and made its way to my ears.

Every hair on my body raised and my steps faltered. I paused in the middle of the passageway, and contemplated turning back. Who knew what kind of magical fate awaited me at the end of the passageway, or what kind of creature could be lurking here in the shadows. Was I being brave, or was I being stupid?

I was about to turn back to rip Apollo from his slumber to follow with me when the voice called to me again.

"Eden hurry." It was a woman's voice, soft and sweet.

It glided smoothly across the air like butter and met my ears. I didn't know why, but my anxiety hadn't flared. Under normal circumstances I was cautious, probably overly, but the voice didn't raise any of my red flags. It only added to the strange sense of de ja vu.

"Hello?" I called back, deciding to go for it.

I couldn't let other people shelter me for my entire life, and I couldn't live it in fear.

Especially not if the fate of my best friend rested on my shoulders.

I rounded the corner and it ended in a dead end, but there was a single exit way. I pressed the button and watched as the wooden slat swung out and slipped through the crack.

What the hell?

I stepped out onto the damp grass, its blades tickling the spaces between my toes.

I turned to see a slab of wood covered in ivy slide back into place against the outside of the manor, camouflaged by all the other ivy that crawled up the outside of the walls.

A chill flowed through me and I tightened my robe at the waist to shelter me from the early morning air.

"Hello?" I whispered into the darkness. All I was met with was the pale moon and the woods that surrounded the manor.

The button to get back inside is going to be a bitch to find underneath all of that ivy. I groaned to myself, ready to give up and see if I could round the corner and sneak back in through the front door when a glint of light shone from the edge of the woods, beckoning to me.

Exploring the manor alone at night was one thing, but exploring the unknown forest alone? That was pushing it, especially for me. But my feet were wet and muddy and I was already cold. I didn't want that to be for nothing.

A large stick poked out from the grass and I picked it up, holding it in my grip tightly. It definitely wasn't anywhere near a proper weapon, and when matched against a mage with any sort of power it wouldn't have protected me even a little bit, but it was the thought that counted. It gave the illusion of safety, and that was something I was willing to buy into if it meant that I would get answers about the mystical light.

I took a step forward. At first it was only an inch, until I gained confidence in the dark enough to walk at my normal pace. I took one last glance at the dark manor over my shoulder before I crossed into the brush of the woods. Up ahead the light was closer now, close enough for me to realize that it had manifested itself in the shape of a woman made of the glow. Her hair flowed effortlessly behind her with each step. It was only an apparition, but I couldn't shake the feeling that I'd been there before, just like the passageway.

I weaved between the trees and made my way over the logs in the worn down pathway. The path had obviously been used throughout the years because the grass had been worn down to nothing but a dirt path, and most of the tree had been cleared to make way for it.

I wondered how many years it had been there for, how many edens had walked it. I could feel the generational magic, it clung to the air like static. it covered everything, even the trees.

I got to the end of the pathway and found myself in a large circular clearing.

In the center stood a stone well, with a bucket perched over top of it. Beside it stood the woman of light. I could see her clearly as she stood waiting for me. She didn't run, and she didn't hide. Which meant the well had to be the final destination. The final stop.

But why a well?

And why in the middle of the forest?

I watched her frame as it stuttered and flowed. She was an apparition, no facial features or distinct marks- except the small symbol that rested where her collar bone would be- a symbol shaped like the scar I had in the same place.

I stared at the mark's black contrast against her otherwise bright white body. My eyes traveled up her body. She was the same height as me, the same build, all the way down to the way she stood leaning partially against the sides of the well.

"Are you, me?" I cocked my head to the side, trying to decipher a way that it could be logically possible but the truth was, there wasn't one.

Just as I was finding was true with a lot of things in the world I lived in, not everything could be explained or proven.

Some things just *were,* and I was slowly coming to accept that.

The woman didn't answer, she simply pointed down into the well. I gazed over its stone wall into the dark waters. It wasn't very deep, but the waters were high. At first I was met with nothing but my own reflection and that of the moon that sat high in the sky above my shoulder. I turned my confused attention back to the apparition, who was absolutely no help.

I didn't understand what she wanted from me.

"Is this why I'm in the middle of the forest at four in the morning?" I asked sarcastically. "What? The water from the tap wasn't good enough or something?" I chuckled at my own joke.

The apparition merely gestured to the well again.

Note to self, magical ghost me doesn't have a sense of humor. Is that how I really come off as? Cold and distant?

I thought about it for a moment, and it made a lot of sense. I had so much anxiety pent up inside me all the time that there were probably times that I seemed like nothing more than a shell on autopilot, trying to shield myself from things I couldn't control.

Point taken. The night had a good reputation for revelations about my life so far.

I turned my attention back to the well where the apparition gestured and concentrated on the water. It was so still that it could have almost been mistaken for a mirror, my reflection unwavering.

Just when I was about to give up, call it a night and find my way back to the kitchen to finish my tea my reflection moved.

It was so subtle that I almost shrugged it off and blamed the sting of my tired eyes.

I cocked my head to the side and furrowed my brow. I watched the reflection do the same and almost breathed a sigh of relief until I straightened my head and my reflection stayed stationary.

My stomach churned and I watched in horror as a maniacal grin spread across my reflections face. She reached her hand out in front of her and beckoned for me to come into the water.

"Two words. Fuck, and No." I shook my head.

I may be a pushover but that was something that I straight up wasn't doing. I was ready to leave this creepy shit show, crawl into the silk sheets, and pray that the traumatizing memory left my mind some time soon when I felt the apparition's hands press against my back and shove me in.

The last thing I remember before fading to black was the rush of cold water.

Chapter 20

I didn't know quite how to describe the whirlwind of senses that came over me as I plunged into the darkness. Inside the well it was pitch black and so cold that I was afraid I'd go into shock. Even with all those things, I didn't feel wet. My skin was as dry as ever and I could breathe just fine.

I went from feeling like I was sinking down to feeling like I was floating up in almost an instant. it was so dark, though, that I couldn't tell the difference. The most unnerving part about the never ending darkness, though, was the reflection- or creature- or whatever the eerie copy of me was called. I couldn't get her twisted smile out of my mind. It reminded me of something straight out of a horror movie.

Just the thought of it made my skin crawl all over again. And I had a bone to pick with that apparition. As soon as I crawled my way out of the well her ass was going in next- magical creature or not.

I couldn't tell if my eyes were open or shut until a dim light shone above my head. I rose higher and higher and the light grew until I was thrown from the well. I shot straight up into the air like a missile and landed stomach first on the harsh forest floor beside it.

My lungs froze up and my entire body tingled with pain. I writhed in the dirt begging my lungs to work again. They sucked in a deep breath and then erupted in a fit of coughing before they even began to work like they should.

I groaned as I pushed myself up to stand, using the rock to steady myself.

Beside the well stood the apparition casually.

"You bitch!" This time I didn't even recoil at the words.

I lunged towards it with my arms out front, ready to shove it down the well for a taste of its own medicine, but I phased right through it stumbling forward like an idiot.

"Of course." I groaned before screaming it again at the sky. "Of course!"

If the apparition was a person I was sure that it would have thought that I was crazy, but lucky for me it was just a mystical menace.

I suddenly realized that the sun hung high in the sky, its hot rays beating down on me.

How long was I in that thing?

Before I could utter another word the apparition turned and began to make its way back down the beaten path. My eyes darted to the path and to the well.

Should I take my chances with the apparition with no manners, or the creepy, evil looking doppelgänger?

I chased after the apparition. It was a no brainer. I knew it would take weeks to even stop seeing the doppelgänger every time I closed my eyes.

The apparition seemed to glide along the path smoothly, even while I stumbled on every rock, stone, and log that I had made my way over on the way to the well.

We emerged from the thicket of trees and the manor came into view. The first thing that caught my eye was the secret door that hung ajar.

An unsettling feeling hung heavily in my stomach, because there was no doubt in my mind that it had closed behind me earlier. I remembered explicitly noticing how well it was hidden among the ivy.

The apparition, however, didn't have a care in the world as she disappeared in the doorway.

Something about it didn't seem right, and it didn't have anything to do with the fact that I was basically taking a house tour from a ghost. It wasn't even about the creepy stunt double that probably sat in the well, waiting to pull me back in.

It was something that hung in the air, something that put me on edge. I could feel my anxiety shoot through the roof and my heart began its familiar thud inside my chest.

I walked through the doorway, and instead of finding myself back in the dark pathway I found myself walking out of the bathroom at the coffee house.

"What the f-"

"Eden!" A voice came from further down the hallway in the dining area.

It was a voice I knew all too well and I cringed at the sound- Veronica. Trent's queen bee, who also happened to think she was queen of the entire world. Her voice reminded me of nails dragging across a chalkboard, high pitched and shrill.

I moved down the hallway toward the voice, and was about to answer her when I noticed a figure across the room- it was me.

I held a mop in my hand, and I stared down at a mess of coffee and shattered glass on the floor.

Veronica and Trent sat at the table that stood beside me, both with smirks across their faces.

"Here's another one for you, while you're at it." Veronica's words seethed with anger as she nudged another coffee filled glass off the edge.

The other me flinched at the crashing sound that cut through the still air.

"What is this?" I said out loud.

"It's you." A woman's voice came from behind me and made the real me jump this time.

I turned around just in time to see her appear from the shadows of the hallway. She was short, and a lot older than me. Her brown hair was streaked with grey, but her face was still slim and defined. She looked so familiar, but I couldn't place her face no matter how hard I tried.

I raised a brow at the smile that crossed her lips. Were those tears dancing in her eyes?

She opened her arms to me and tears streamed down her face.

I stood awkwardly and raised a brow at her.

"You don't know who I am?" She tried to mask the hurt in her voice.

"Part of my drowning hallucination?"

She let her arms fall at her sides, a look of hurt on her face. "That's okay. I don't know why I thought you would. You were only three when we had to send you away."

Her words shook me. It couldn't be true. "You're my moth-" I caught myself and rushed to rephrase. "- the woman who gave me up?"

I'd hoped that she hadn't caught on to the word that I fumbled over, but the hurt in her eyes made it obvious that she had.

She averted her eyes back to the scene that was unfolding behind me, and my eyes followed hers. We watched as the other version of me bent over and picked the shards of broken glass out of the mess. The look on her- I mean my- face was just as broken as the glasses were.

"I waited so long for this moment. Over the years I prayed that one day I'd get a glimpse at what my baby girl was like."

I rolled my eyes. "You would have known if you hadn't given me up."

She disregarded my words and continued on her train of thought. "But I have to admit, this isn't who I thought I'd be meeting. Why do you let people treat you like that?" Her tone wasn't shameful, it sounded like it was an actual question.

And it wasn't one I had the answers to.

It became obvious that this was some sort of magical hallucination caused by the well, but why? Why make me watch my life from the outside?

I had to admit it was hard to stomach. I watched Veronica whisper about me to Trent while I mopped up the mess she had intentionally made. I watched as my double cocked her head to the side slightly. She caught what they had said, what they were laughing so ferociously about, but she didn't say a word.

While that situation in particular hadn't really happened, it was a perfect mirror for others that had throughout my life.

"It's a mirror." I mumbled.

"What was that?" My mother asked.

"The well. It's a mirror, right? Made to make me see things that I couldn't see from the inside."

My mother smirked, and I felt a small twinge of pride at the sight of her being impressed.

"It's the well of truth, meant to uncover a side of someone that they can't admit to themselves." Her voice was soft. "Did the apparition lead you here?"

I rolled my eyes and half grinned. "I swear when I get my hands on that thing it's going headfirst in this god damned thing."

My mother smiled. "That's it. That's the glimmer of me that I was hoping I'd see." She held out her hand for a handshake, probably still pining for any form of human contact with me.

"Devina." She said with a firm shake. "Montgomery."

"Eden." I nodded, only to kick myself a millisecond later. "But you know that, because you gave me that name."

She laughed.

"So, how'd you get from that, to this." She gestured from the scene behind to me.

I mulled over the question. I guess I still saw myself as the girl on the floor, always rushing to pick up other peoples shards, apologizing like I was the one who broke the glass in the first place.

But seeing it from the outside I realized how much I'd not only outgrown that girl, but felt sad for her. After everything I'd been through, the blaze of fire I felt inside it was hard for me to imagine ever letting anyone treat me like that again.

"I don't know." I murmured.

I caught a glimpse of the apparition by the front door, waiting for me.

"That's my ride." I moved to the door and Devina followed.

"Mine too."

A sense of awkwardness shuddered through me. Did I really want this spell, or whatever the hell it was, showing all of my shortcomings and weaknesses in front of her?

I barely knew the woman, and Apollo had said she was dead. Was she real? Was she part of my subconscious?

Maybe she was part of the spell itself, one of the biggest blindspots that I needed to work to overcome- being abandoned by the people who were supposed to love me the most.

I shoved through the door and found myself standing in the living room of the house Jade and I shared. It was warm and cozy, just like it always had been.

In front of us Jade and Charles snuggled on the couch and watched a movie. I sat awkwardly in an armchair off to the side- alone. Every once in a while my eyes darted to the couple and back to the screen, a longing in my eyes.

"Okay okay I get it. I want love but won't let myself accept it." I huffed to the apparition. "Can we move on to the next one?" My cheeks were warm, and I avoided looking in Devina's eyes.

Without a word the apparition moved to the small doorway that led to the coat closet and I followed closely behind.

The familiar smell of chlorine stung my nose, something I shivered at every time I crossed its place.

No. A wave of fear spread through me as I realized where we were- the pool at my old academy.

Chapter 21

"Okay I want to leave." I spun around to rush back through the doorway but walked right into the solid tiled wall.

Fuck.

My eyes watered, and I was at least glad that I could blame that on the impact of the wall, but in all honestly it had nothing to do with it.

I turned to watch, paralyzed by fear as I saw the tiny version of me standing on the diving board. Behind me the nuns stood with a yardstick, poking me in the back inching me closer to the depth of water.

I watched the tears stream down my little face with every inch of safety that I lost from the water.

"No, stop." I said- a pathetic attempt.

Warm tears streamed down my own cheeks, and a familiar wave of emotional exhaustion fell over me. I was getting ready to shut down, to retreat back into myself.

Then it dawned on me.

"No one ever stuck up for me." My words started out as a mumble before erupting into a yell. "No one ever stuck up for me! Not even myself." The words were hot with magic as they left my lips.

"You left me here, with them." I pointed a finger at Devina. "You left me, and they pounded it into my head over and over that nobody wanted me. No one stuck up for me, and it taught me not to even bother sticking up for myself!" I unleashed years of hatred, and anger, and pain. It came spewing out of my mouth in the form of a magical white mist, nearly identical to the mist that made up the apparition. The room around us shook violently, but I was so consumed in a fit of emotion that I didn't even notice.

Devina just smiled. Not sarcastically, or egotistically, but sincere.

"That was it." She said. "That was what's been holding you back.

Around us the room faded away, until it disappeared into black and another scene came into view.

I felt a weight lift off my shoulders. I'd let go of a burden that I didn't even know I'd been carrying my whole life. I didn't just feel free- I felt empowered.

There wasn't an ounce of anxiety left inside me. I was brand new, from the inside out.

The Temple of Eden materialized around us, and we found ourselves standing inside the main corridor.

"Is that, us?" My eyes fell on a younger version of Devina.

She cradled me in her arms. I clung to a tattered old blanket and the look on my face was content- I was the only one. Devina and my father looked terrified.

"How do you know they're coming?" Devina's voice was a low whisper. She tightened her grip on me.

"Because I know. We don't have a lot of time." I watched as my father rushed to Apollo's temple door, and opened it with ease before doing the same with Asher's. "I'm going to collect all the scrolls and send them with you both. Don't open them until you're far away from here."

There was pain laced in his voice.

"But I want you to come with us daddy." I tugged at his shirt.

"I know sweetie, but daddy has to take care of something, okay? Then I'll meet you and mommy and we'll run away together. Okay?"

"You mean the bad guys?" My double asked, with her big brown eyes wide.

My father's eyes darted up to Devina and she shrugged. "She's your daughter! She hears everything!"

Beside me, the older Devina chuckled and shook her head.

My eyes darted back to my father.

"Yes honey, but everything's going to be okay. Okay?"

Before he could fit in another word Johnathon rushed inside.

"They're here sir."

"Already? No this isn't supposed to-" My father looked down at me and cut his sentence short.

"No. Don't do it." Devina snapped at him. "There has to be another way."

"There isn't." My father disappeared into Asher's tomb, unlocked the chest, and brought back the scroll before handing it to me.

"Hey peach." He said with tears in his eyes.

Tears filled mine at the sentiment.

"Hey."

"Daddy is going to give you something super duper important, okay? I need to make sure that you take care of it, and don't use it until you're ready."

"Is it that?" Tiny me pointed at the rolled up scroll, but my father shook his head.

"This is important too, but I have something even more special. Okay? But before that I need you to know I love you. I will never ever stop loving you. Never forget how great you are." He pulled my little body in for a hug before placing his hand over my collar bone- right over my scar.

The room shook and my father writhed in pain. He threw his head back and I realized his eyes were just two beams of light. He became consumed by the mystical glowing light and I screamed, but the sound was drowned out by the building shaking. Before my eyes my father evaporated in front of me, leaving nothing but a white mist that entered me through the fresh mark underneath my collarbone.

Tears streamed down my little cheeks and tumbled to the ground.

An explosion erupted outside.

"You need to go, now Devina! They've seen you. They know you exist. She's still a secret, and if she can stay that way she'll live." Johnathon urged her.

She swooped me up, I was a sobbing mess, and the scroll slipped from my fingertips.

"No! Daddy gave me that!" I managed to sneak the words out between my sobs, but there wasn't time to turn around.

It was then or never.

I turned to look at the real Devina, or whatever the one beside me was. I saw her with fresh eyes.

"Leaving you was the hardest thing I ever had to do." She managed to get the words out. "But you heard him. They knew I existed. They didn't have a clue that you did. I lost your father, I wasn't about to let them take you too."

I pulled Devina in for a hug, half expecting to phase through her like I had the apparition but I didn't. She was solid. I squeezed her tightly.

The old Eden would have cringed at the human contact. She would have overanalyzed and felt awkward the entire time, but after everything that I'd seen I could honestly say that I wasn't that version of her anymore. And I didn't plan to go back.

My father's words stuck with me.

Never forget how great you are.

I didn't have any memories of him, but I could tell by the few moments that he was the best father ever. And somewhere inside me, the magic that had coursed through his veins coursed through mine too. I wasn't going to let that go in vain.

Around us the world began to crumble. The apparition dispersed into an orb of magic that surrounded Devina and I.

"What's happening?" I asked.

"You're bringing me home." Devina said with a smile. "Before any of this happened your father brought me to a powerful witch and had a second chance spell placed on me. He had a feeling that something would happen, and when it did the spells magic carried my soul to the magical waters of the well- the same waters used to preserve the lives of the water spectres that live in the manor. And you, my love, have just awoken me."

At her words the orb ascended into the air, leaving the world around us in darkness. We both shot out of the top of the well and tumbled to the ground in a heap.

Devina sat straight up in the growing morning light and the sun glinted across her glistening blue figure- she was made of water just like the rest of them.

"You're made of water now." I said in awe.

"I don't even care, not as long as I get to be there to make up for all the years that were lost. I knew I can never bring those back, but I'm here to watch you kick ass now."

She brought me in for a hug and for the first time in my life I felt like everything was going to be okay.

***

I rubbed at my eyes tiredly. I had already snuck Devina back into the house, and was on my way to try to get any amount of sleep that the universe was willing to send me when the urge hit me like a freight train.

I was going to tell Apollo where he could shove it.

After my night of self exploration, and my father's lasting words I had come to the conclusion that I was done letting Apollo make me feel like shit.

I knocked on his bedroom door, and out of habit anticipated the flutters of anxiety in my stomach. To my surprise all I felt was a rush of adrenaline.

Behind the door I could hear him crawling out of his bed and sleepily dragging his feet to the door.

"Eden?" He said rubbing the sleep from his eyes and stifling a yawn.

"You can't treat me like shit anymore." I said barging past him and into his room.

The look of confusion across his face was priceless.

"Excuse me?" He shut the door and ran his fingers through his hair.

I could see his groggy brain trying to process what the hell I was talking about, so I decided to spell it out for him. Loud and clear.

"I'm sick of you pushing me around and making me feel like shit. This on again, off again, you're my fated mate but I don't want anything to do with you bullshit is done with. Now. I'm not taking anymore of it. Like fuck, you don't have to love me just because some random magic says you do, but you do have to accept that magic ties us together and respect me."

I tried not to pant after the long winded message.

Apollo's mouth hung open, and a sense of satisfaction flowed through me.

It felt good to be free from my anxiety. Really good. I didn't ever want to go back to the way I was before.

"Well, are you going to say some-"

My words were cut off as Apollo rushed to me and wrapped his arms around me tightly pressing his lips against mine. He kissed me, for the second time ever, with a passion that burned so hot that I could feel it too. I didn't know what was going on, but I didn't care. It melted into the kiss and the sexual tension that had always filled the room when Apollo entered melted too. It was only him, and I. In that moment nothing else mattered.

His arms locked behind me, squeezing me closely into his body, and I interlocked my fingers behind his neck.

Apollo pulled away and looked deep into my eyes. "How could I ever do anything but love your stubborn ass?"

The words sounded foreign coming from his mouth, like there was an entire deep side to Apollo that I was only just seeing.

I pulled him into me this time. His warm tongue slid into my mouth and flicked against mine as I stumbled backward onto his bed. Apollo crawled over me, and his lips found their way to my neck, hitting a sweet spot behind my ear that I didn't even know existed. With every kiss he planted I felt my panties get wetter and wetter. My clit ached, begging for attention.

I'd never had sex before, but I knew that it was what my body was craving. I didn't just want Apollo inside of me- I needed it. More than I needed air or water.

Apollo's lips brushed against the scar on my collarbone and sent an electric shiver down my spine that rested between my legs.

I pulled him in for a kiss and my hand traveled down his chest to the bulge in his pants. His thin pajamas didn't have a chance at holding back his rock hard cock, and as my fingers brushed against the huge bulge my eyes widened. His dick was a lot bigger than I had expected, but somehow the challenge only turned me on even more.

At the touch of my hand through the cloth something awakened inside of Apollo. A sexual hunger that demanded to be satisfied.

He looked deep into my eyes before sliding my tank top over my head and shimmying me out of my pajama bottoms and panties.

There I lay in the bed, exposed and naked, his for the taking.

And I'd never wanted anyone to take me more than I wanted him to.

Apollo slid two fingers in his mouth before bringing them to my dripping wet pussy. He traced my lips with his fingertips and waves of pleasure coursed through my clit, making me arch my back. If this felt that good I couldn't imagine how good it would feel to have his thick cock spread me open.

He started to insert a fingertip but stopped when he felt resistance.

His eyes met mine with a sexual curiosity.

"Are you a virgin?"

I nodded and sunk my teeth into my bottom lip. "But in a few minutes I won't be."

Apollo didn't ask questions, he just climbed out of his pajama pants and poised himself on top of me, resting between my legs. It was a beautiful sight, his chiseled abs and his rock hard cock, standing at attention for me. A drop of precum glistened at the tip, and I shivered at the thought of it inside of me. I wanted so badly to know how it felt, every drop of it, filling my sacred hole- one no man had ever explored.

"Are you ready?"

I nodded eagerly and relaxed my body. I felt the head of his dick spread the lips of my pussy open and I was gushing wet with anticipation. He thrust in slowly, inch by inch. A pinch of pain mixed in with the ecstasy of pleasure as he slid in as far as he could before he reached my hymen. The cherry on my pussy sundae that hadn't, and wouldn't be, enjoyed by anyone but him. You only get one cherry, and I was ready for him to pop the fuck out of mine.

He hesitated, so I shimmied my hips, thrusting them at him and forcing the full length of this throbbing cock inside of me. A wave of pleasurable pain erupted inside me as my body learned to open up parts of me that had never been opened before.

Apollo pulled all the way out and slowly thrust himself inside of me again, this time a little faster.

A sexy smirk crossed my face.

"That time it didn't hurt as much." I half moaned.

"Oh yeah? How about this?" Apollo pulled out and shoved his dick back inside me a little faster, a soft moan escaping his lips.

"That one hurt even less." I closed my eyes and moaned.

Apollo took that as a sign that it was okay to fuck me however he wanted, and he did a glorious job. His mouth found my nipple and he sunk his teeth into it while his cock rammed inside of me, hitting my G-spot.

I had no idea that sex would feel that good, otherwise I would have been having a hell of a lot more of it.

"Holy shit, holy shit, holy shit." I moaned as a bubbling feeling erupted between my legs and I looked up at him.

In that moment Apollo was raw, real, and transparent. He pulled me in for the kiss of all kisses, kissing me long and hard. It was almost passionate enough for me to forget all the times he had ever been a dick.

All that mattered now was *his* dick.

I reveled in the feeling of it stretching me from the inside out.

I gasped and I felt my body tense up, my back arching in orgasmic bliss. Fireworks erupted inside of my mind and I felt my pussy tighten, massaging his cock just enough to push him over the edge of pleasure.

He thrust inside me as far as he could and I felt the gush of his hot cum fill me. He collapsed beside me, pulling his dick out and panting heavily.

I tried to keep my eyes open. There were so many things I

wanted to say to him, but after everything that had happened I was too far past exhausted to be saved.

I felt Apollo's lips press against my forehead and I slipped into the comforting darkness of sleep.

Chapter 22

My eyelids slowly fluttered open, thoroughly convinced that being awoken by the tantalizing scent of fresh bacon is the best way to do so.

I sat up and winced. A twinge of discomfort rested between my legs as proof that I hadn't imagined the entire night with Apollo. A small smile curled my lips at the thought. It was like I could still feel his cock inside of me, and when I was going to feel it again was definitely on my mind, but the smell of bacon overpowered all else. I sat up and yawned with nothing but the bedspread to cover me.

I turned to wake Apollo but he was already gone.

"Good morning to you too." I mumbled as I slipped into my pajamas and set out to find the source of the delicious smell.

I made my way into the hallway and I couldn't help but notice I felt different. It was like I was seeing things out of new eyes. I was in the same house, but everything bathed in a more positive light than it had the day before.

I was actually *happy,* not to mention excited to see what the day would bring- and it wasn't just because I wasn't carrying my V-card anymore. It was a mixture of things, starting with the answers about my past, and ending with the new sense of confidence and determination that I felt.

I made my way into the kitchen, rubbing at my eyes with a balled fist. I was surprised to see Devina's shimmering figure sitting at the table, alongside all three guys. They all spun around, eyes glued to me as I walked in.

"You brought your mom back from the dead?" A smile spread across Adler's face. "I told you you were fucking cool."

I laughed.

"I guess I know there's no keeping a good secret in this house."

I pulled a jug of orange juice from the refrigerator and poured a glass.

Everyone turned back to Devina. She was telling some story about my father and his power but at that point I was so close to the bacon that I couldn't bring myself to think of much else.

Johnathon handed me a plate of bacon, eggs, and pancakes and I nearly drooled all over it. I couldn't even remember the last time that I'd eaten a proper meal. it felt like the last few days I'd only survived on the grace of the gods themselves, and magic.

My body was only now remembering what the hell food was, and I was happy to say it was a tear filled reunion.

I took a seat at the table beside Devina and the guys and drowned my pancakes in syrup before devouring them all. I looked up to see Adler staring directly at me.

"And you can handle a stack of pancakes." He smirked. "I changed my mind, I'm officially in love."

I kicked him underneath the table and he laughed.

"So, I was thinking today I could work on mastering your elements." I said, unintentionally cutting off Devina.

I didn't mean to rush into it, but the truth was since I'd seen my father, and closed the gaping holes in my heart that my traumas had left, it was like I could finally feel the magic coursing through me. It was a faint hum, but it was there nonetheless, and I couldn't wait to put it to the test.

The guys all shifted their attention to me, their eyes hungry and eager.

What did I get myself into?

***

The warm sun beat down on my face, so much so that I opted to slip out of my robe, leaving me in nothing but my tank top and pajama bottoms.

"When I said I wanted to train, I kind of meant later. You know when I had a shower and maybe a fresh set of clothes." I shielded my face with my hand just enough to see Atlas standing in front of me.

"Magic waits for no one. Not even a face like yours." Atlas said with a smirk.

His white teeth glistened in the sunlight and I flashed a sarcastic smile in return.

We stood in the clearing in the back of the manor that sat between the temple and the house. On the sidelines sat Devina, Apollo, and Adler perched in lawn chairs like they were about to watch their favorite sport.

"Okay, okay, just tell me what I have to do." I said.

I'd barely gotten the words from my mouth when Atlas threw a football as hard as he could. It zipped at me faster than I could catch it and it hit me square in the temple. A wall of pain came with it, crashing into the side of my head.

I crumpled to the ground and cradled my face in my hands.

"What the hell was that!" I yelled.

I looked up just in time to see a soccer ball hurling towards me, but two seconds too late for me to stop it. It hit me in the head too.

"Fuck!" I yelled angrily.

On the sidelines Apollo and Adler snickered.

"You need to use air to stop it, honey." My mother called out.

"Thanks for the advice." My eyes snapped to her shimmering blue figure.

I got to my feet and just as I did I saw a dodgeball spiraling toward my face. My arm shot up and I winced as it bounced off my forearm. "I don't know what this has to do with anything!" I seethed, an anger building in me.

My head throbbed and my arm ached, and in that moment all I wanted was to pumble his handsome face.

"Please, you have it easy, my father used knives." Atlas half laughed.

"Mine used swords." Adler raised his hand.

"Rocks." My eyes darted to Apollo.

And I thought my family was messed up. I huffed.

"Okay okay I get it. But don't you think you should actually teach me something before hurling random objects at me?"

"No. In all reality you're more powerful than all of us combined. You just need to find the right motivation." Atlas shrugged before lifting a metal shovel.

I took one look at the point that sat at the end and shook my head.

"Nope. I draw the line at that. You can't be serious."

Atlas's eyes went completely white as he called on his power to command the wind. A gust of air flowed from his hand making the shovel hover .

"I'm dead serious."

With that the gust of wind shot the shovel fast like a missile, sending it straight through the air- but not at me.

The shovel soared through the air headed straight for Devina and my heart sank.

I wasn't very well versed in the magical properties of water spectres. I had no idea if they were immortal, or even if they felt pain. What I did know was that I'd just gotten my mother back. She had a lot of missed years to make up for, and I was actually looking forward to all the ass kissing she was going to have to do to accomplish it.

Around me time slowed and it felt like every inch of my body began to vibrate. I was consumed by the sensation of pins and needles inching up my arms. There was so much power stuck inside me, begging to be released.

"No!" I screamed, flinging my arms out in the direction of the shovel.

A burst of air exploded from my palms releasing a deafening boom and collided with the handle knocking it off course, sparing my mother from her fate.

The flow of energy from my hands was so powerful that the pressure of its release blasted me backward and sent me skidding to a halt on my back.

My arms throbbed and my ears rang. A groan escaped my lips, and all three guys rushed over to me. Atlas's eyes had returned to their normal mesmerizing grey, and he still held his signature smirk across his lips.

"See, I told you you could do it."

He offered me a hand and I gladly took it. I was pulled to my feet and brushed the skids of grass from my tank top when I noticed Atlas took a seat and Adler had stepped forward.

"Please don't tell me you're here to throw things at me, because I think Atlas already chucked everything but the kitchen sink."

Adler laughed and my heart jumped at the sound. There was something about hearing it escape my lips that made me happy. It was always so genuine, never forced. And it was contagious. It made me think of the moment we'd shared the night before, all the laughs.

"No, you know I like to play games, so I have one for you."

I raised a brow.

A game seemed easy enough.

He picked up a stick off the ground and held it out.

"All you have to do is take this stick. As soon as you do, you win."

It sounded too good to be true, and I had no idea what it had to do with learning how to navigate my earth magic, but who was I to complain?

I casually strolled across the field to Adler and reached for the outstretched stick. A fraction of a second before my hands could wrap around it a root shot out from the ground, wrapped around my ankle, and hoisted me in the air, leaving me hanging upside down.

My tank top flew above my head, flashing Adler, which he was very clearly excited about.

"Did you like the show?" I groaned sarcastically as I pulled my shirt back down and the root lowered me to the ground.

"I did actually, but I'm still waiting for a challenge." Adler faked a yawn and scratched his back with the stick.

Inside me a fire blazed.

If he wanted a challenge, he was about to get one.

I got up and rushed at him, quicker this time, but a root emerged from the ground and snagged my foot sending me spiraling back to the unforgiving ground.

I gritted my teeth in frustration. I was just settling into my newfound confidence, I wasn't going to let a little defeat rid me of it.

Adler laughed as I lay at his feet, and the determination inside of me only grew.

I closed my eyes and thought about what Atlas had said. The magic wasn't only magic, it was alive. It had chosen me to wield it, that included the earth.

I threaded my fingers in with the grass and quieted my mind, allowing me to tune into the hum of the soil. With a single thrust of my energy three large roots shot out from the ground. Two tangled themselves around Adler's arms rendering him immobile, and one wrapped around the stick. It ripped it from his grasp and placed it in my hands.

With a knowing smirk I pulled myself to stand and twirled it in the air.

"What was that about a challenge?"

The roots set Adler free and rescinded into the ground. I didn't want to jinx it, but I finally felt like I was getting a handle on my magic. They were small moves, but they were still moves in the right direction.

Just when Apollo stood and was about to present his challenge Johnathon's voice came from beside the building.

"Miss Eden, you need to hear this. Now!"

We all exchanged worried glances before rushing into the manor.

"What? What?" I said between pants.

Johnathon motioned to a beat up police radio that sat on the fireplace mantel in the living room.

"We have it on from time to time, because what other excitement are we going to get? And we heard this."

He flipped the switch and a burst of static erupted from the speaker until a voice came through.

"I repeat, we have multiple fires across the city, and a fire mage holding a girl hostage on top of a residence- over."

"Jade." I gasped.

Chapter 23

Our small town car hit a bump in the road and was almost sent soaring because of how fast Apollo was driving. He punched his foot down on the gas pedal and we were sent speeding into town. I would have been afraid of getting pulled over if it wasn't so obvious that they had bigger fish to fry.

My jaw hung open as the buildings of the small town I'd lived in came into view. It was utter chaos. Multiple buildings on both sides of the street were up in flames. People poured out of the doors of shops and restaurants as the fire spread. Crowds rushed up and down the street, erupting in fits of frantic screaming and crying.

"What the hell happened to the water caste?" Adler's low voice came from the back seat.

"Asher happened." It was so surreal that I almost couldn't believe what I was seeing. The place that I'd called home for most of my life was on its way to becoming nothing but ruins. Ashes of what it once was. "Was he always this fucking murderous?"

The words came out hot and angry. I couldn't imagine how anyone could bring themselves to be so evil, and better yet how the universe had paired me with someone like that. Why would I spark with someone who held such a deep hatred for the world that they were capable of such harsh destruction.

"No." Apollo murmured. We turned a corner and he tightened his grip on the steering wheel. "He was my best friend once."

So much pain and anguish hid between his words. "Growing up we did everything together. He was gentle then, even softer than Adler."

"Hey!" Adler protested from the back.

"But when we hit puberty, and were given our full carrier powers something inside of him changed. It was like the darkness inside him started to seep out- when his parents were killed he just lost it. His uncle took over as the fire caste's sorcerer and whispered things in his ear. He planted the extremist ideas in his head that the fire caste should be the ones to rule, and at a time when Asher desperately needed something to believe in he caved."

As we inched closer to my old house the words sunk in.

If it was his uncle pulling the strings before, who's pulling the strings now?

There were still so many things that I didn't know. So many questions left unanswered, and I felt like Devina could help us bridge some of the gaps.

"That's the thing with fire magic." Atlas added from the back seat. "It's the most potent, most chaotic element of all. There are stories throughout history of the mages it's power had been bestowed to losing their minds, going off the deep end, maybe even going mad all together."

I sunk my teeth into my bottom lip.

Was that going to happen to me? I was just settling into my new skin, learning to be comfortable with myself the way I was. Was it a possibility that unlocking the fire element inside of me would send me down the rabbit hole of an even deeper personality change?

There was only one way to tell- by actually unlocking it, and I didn't know if that was going to happen any time soon.

As we sped through the burning city we passed a lot of fire trucks, all scattered about amongst the streets that were engulfed in flames.

I watched as a team of firefighters magically pulled a stream of water from a hydrant up ahead. It took six of them to even pull out a decent amount, and they were fighting a losing battle.

Inside the house a mother dangled her baby out the second story window, pleading for someone to catch him. I could see the deep shade of fear in her face all the way from the car.

"Pull over Apollo." I demanded.

"If I pull over we might not make it to Jade in time." He answered, his eyes still locked on the road in front of us.

"I said pull over!" I yanked the steering wheel from his grip and the car jerked to the right, sending the car halfway up the curb.

Before I could even fill the guys in on what I was doing I leaped from the car.

Once again time began to slow around me, and an icy feeling spread across my eyes as they turned completely white.

Listen to the wind. I took a deep breath and calmed my mind. My arms welcomed the tingling feeling that was slowly becoming a familiar sensation and I forced it out- my hands at my sides with my palms turned upright. In front of me a small gust of wind began to swirl. I watched as it grew and grew before becoming a small tornado. I guided it to the window and the force was so strong it swept the mother and her baby from the window. I used every ounce of concentration I could to set them gently on the sidewalk. Everyone turned to look at me in awe, the firefighters, the woman, even the guys- but I wasn't done yet.

I knew that somewhere inside of me I held the power to command water, my fear was the only thing holding me back.

And at that moment I didn't have time to feel fear, and whatever minuscule amounts I did feel were subsequently drowned out by the rush of adrenaline that spidered it's way through my veins.

The water that poured out of the fire hydrant faltered and the stream that the firefighters were working to collectively lift began to ripple. With a loud bang the entire fire hydrant came unbolted and landed on the sidewalk across the street, leaving a crater beneath it. I focused my energy on the huge gush of water that flowed from the hole it left behind and forced it on the burning building, with a smile plastered on my face.

The firefighters erupted in applause and the woman's eyes teared up as she mouthed a thank you.

I slipped back into the car and all three of the guys stared at me.

"Fast learner." Atlas slapped the back of the seat and Apollo threw the car back into gear speeding off.

We rounded the final corner and the car came screeching to a halt. The entire street was a circus of cop cars and swat vehicles. Everything was up in flames. If I hadn't known better I would have thought that it was the beginning of the end- the apocalypse finally catching up to us.

But the second my eyes locked onto the roof of the house I knew that there was something else aloof.

"Jade." The word came out nearly a whisper.

On top of the house stood Asher. He stood behind Jade with his arm around her shoulder, holding her tightly to him. I flipped the hood on my sweater up and jumped from the car. It was the only defense I had against people seeing my face. The last thing I needed was for the cops to get a glimpse of me and opt to slap another pair of cuffs on my wrists.

The guys trailed closely behind me as I weaved through the crowd of growing spectators that lined the sidewalks. Their houses and businesses were up in flames, but what they opted to stare at was the girl being held captive?

Once again a fit of anger sturred in the pit of my stomach- at Asher, at the Spectators, at the world.

It was like all the anger I'd suppressed for years decided to bubble to the surface, and my face blazed hot. I couldn't tell if it was from the flames that nearly surrounded us or if the fire magic inside me was beginning to activate, but I didn't much care anymore.

I was angry at everything that had a pulse, everything that breathed, the entire universe.

Up ahead some cops closed in, stepping foot in our yard and attempting to charge into the house, presumably to get to the roof and take down Asher- bad idea.

The second their feet crossed the threshold into the yard a stream of molten fire spewed from Asher's palms, turning every officer into a pile of ash.

The look in his eye was delirious.

I managed to push past the officer in charge of crowd control as he was turning to hold back the guys.

"Get out of there kid!" An officer yelled from behind me as I stepped foot in the yard.

No officer dared to follow me.

Asher reached out, about to set me ablaze before he realized who I was and an evil grin graced his lips.

"Finally!" He yelled. "What does it take for a guy to get your attention? I mean come on, I burned down half of this god forsaken place already. I was beginning to think that you'd never show and poor Jadey and I were going to be here all alone."

He pulled her closer to his body.

My eyes landed on Jade's. She looked worn down and tired, but she still managed to force a smile.

I tried to tell her with my eyes- tell her that I'd never stopped looking for her. That I wasn't going to stop until she was safe.

I wished that I could tell her all the things I'd done, how my life had changed, how much I'd grown.

But in that moment all I could do was force half of a smile back.

"What do you want?" I yelled back. "I'll do anything, just let her go."

"Anything?" Asher asked with a glint in his eye.

"Anything."

"Okay, it's simple- I want you dead." His demand was clear.

My eyes flitted to Jades, and I noticed the fear woven into them. My childhood best friend- she was the girl who took a chance on the poor orphan even when she was the most popular girl in school, the girl the old Eden would have literally died for if given a chance. But old me didn't have the newfound purpose in life. She didn't know where she fit, or who she loved, or who loved her, so it would have been an easy choice.

But now, I couldn't go down- especially not without a fight.

"Okay, I lied. Anything else." I smiled sarcastically.

I felt the icy feeling in my eyes return as they melted into white. Beneath me I conjured the power of a small whirlwind that lifted me into the sky. Around me lightning bolts shot, connecting with the grass and leaving behind nothing but smoldering scorch marks.

"Okay, you want to do this the hard way." I said, fully prepared to unleash all of my abilities on Asher.

We shared a spark, but that wasn't going to stop me from killing him. I was willing to go as far as I had to. I wasn't leaving the city without Jade, I couldn't let her down again.

"That's funny, I was about to say the same thing to you." In an instant Asher reached up, placed his hands on either side of Jade's face, and twisted her neck.

I watched her body crumple to the roof in a still heap, limp and unmoving.

My eyes returned to normal and I felt like all the air had been sucked out of my lungs as I spiraled to the harsh ground.

Tears streamed from my eyes and ran down my cheeks in two trails as the overwhelming sense of grief hit me all at once. I was so consumed with the shock of it that I shut down, reverting into a sobbing heap.

I collapsed to my knees and screamed at the top of my lungs. It was such an ear piercing sound that, mixed with the release of my air magic, shattered every window in the house, not to mention every building on the street.

Behind me the crowd of people screamed and shielded themselves for the shards that rained down. Out of the corner of my eye I could see them finally starting to scatter, sheltering themselves.

They really stood there and watched the city that they loved burn to the ground but *I* was the monster that they were afraid of?

My grief mixed with disgust at the world. Was it even worth saving anymore?

From atop the roof Asher began to rain fire down at me when Apollo, Atlas, and Adler jumped in between us. They combined their three types of magic. Apollo created a water beam to push back against the fire. Adler commanded vines to creep up the side of the house, and Atlas created a reverse portal of air to suck some of the oxygen from the flames, causing them to die down.

The three of them together were a decent match for Asher but his power was different from theirs, his was fueled by angst and hatred. Those were two things that I could tell he had plenty of, and thus his power was potent. They were losing ground, and they were losing ground fast.

Just when I was about to give up and let Asher put me out of my misery I noticed something move up on the roof with Asher, it was Jade.

She sat straight up and Asher shot her an angry glare.

"You're too early babe, fuck!"

I saw her mouth the word *oops*.

"Babe?" The word left a sour taste in my mouth. I pulled myself to stand, my sobbing slowed. "Jade, you're okay?"

"Well I guess the cat's out of the bag now." Jade threw her hands up and groaned as she stood next to Asher.

"Because you couldn't play dead long enough!" He blamed.

"Well you said that you'd kill her right away and I wouldn't have to!" She whined, slipping a long strand of blonde hair behind her ear.

"What the fuck is going on?" I felt my fists clench tightly at my sides.

The more my brain processed the more my stomach churned.

She was in on it.

"Are you two fucking sleeping together?" I seethed.

Asher had stopped his rain of fire to embrace Jade, slipping his arm around her waist with one arm while he still held a ball of fire in the other, ready to throw at a moment's notice.

"Wow, she got really ballsy while she was away." Jade snorted.

I had witnessed her bitchy side before. She was ruthless with other girls, but she'd always told me she'd never be that way to me. She swore she didn't talk that way behind my back, but in that moment I wasn't so sure anymore.

The more time that went by the more pieces of my heart slowly shattered.

"You're joking. This is a joke." I said through gritted teeth.

"At first when he kidnapped me, it was real. But look at him, he's too hot to be stuck with and *not* sleep with." Jade flipped her hair over her shoulder. "I'm sorry Eden, but the only joke here is you. What did you think was going to happen? You were going to sweep in and save the world? *You*?"

The pieces of my broken heart fell into my stomach and bubbled into a voracious anger.

Inside me something broke. It was like a glowstick, dark until I snapped and a hot wave of fire magic seeped out filling me up. It burned every inch of my body, even resting behind my eyes.

Asher noticed and began to rain fire down on me again, but it was too late- I was a magical bomb and I'd gone atomic.

Every inch of my body glowed a bright shade of orange.

"You're really going to regret that." I managed to squeeze the words out as every inch of my body vibrated.

The heat built up inside me until it had nowhere to go. It exploded out with a deafening boom and a wave of fire blasted out in every direction. I felt the earth beneath me cave in, and I slipped back into the familiar darkness with one last thought on my mind.

No one will ever underestimate me again.

STORM SONG

Manufactured by Amazon.ca
Bolton, ON